THEIR ONLY PATH TO SURVIVAL

PURSUIT
OF PERIL

MARLYS & ISAAC ADLER

Published by Zaccmedia
www.zaccmedia.com
info@zaccmedia.com

Published June 2021

Paperback ISBN: 978-1-911211-77-8

British Library Cataloguing-in-Publication Data
A catalogue record for this book is available from the British Library

Cover design & typesetting by Paul Stanier

This book is dedicated to those who lost their lives yet remain a living testament to the heart and soul of Israel. Their story will be passed down through generations.

PROLOGUE

It was the late 1930s. Hitler and his armies were storming Europe. Follow the sequence of events as Benjamin (Benny) Goldberg, along with other volunteers, agrees to become part of a clandestine mission, designed by a determined Jewish leadership, to rescue as many Jews as possible and bring them to Palestine—at that time still under British rule.

While encouraging others to believe in themselves and their future, Benny struggles with his own feelings of compassion and anger during a mission gone awry.

This dramatic historical novel evokes a wide range of emotions as we are introduced to the Jewish refugees involved and become a part of their lives. Their resilience while struggling on this perilous pursuit of survival on both land and sea—along with the shocking outcome—is a true testament to the human spirit.

This is their story.

1

DAVID'S SPEECH

Benny says goodbye to Varda and leaves, joining the others who are attending what they have been told is to be a very important meeting. More than a dozen men and women crowd into the small front room of a second-floor apartment, located a short walking distance from the beach in the heart of Tel Aviv. Cigarette smoke hangs like a cloud of gray mist in the hot, humid air.

Light, good-natured bantering was always a part of these gatherings. They were not something new; only locations for the meetings varied, in keeping with the British government's tight control on everything going on in Palestine these days.

After finding out who tonight's guest speaker is, conversations in the room take on a more serious tone. David Ben-Gurion had a reputation for being an unyielding force in the ongoing movement for the preservation of Jews.

A very recognizable David enters the room. He maneuvers through the welcoming handshakes, giving a friendly pat on the back to those nearest him as he makes his way to the front of the group. Looking around the room, he begins to speak without ceremony.

"Let me tell you why we're here tonight. You all know our brothers and sisters throughout Europe are under the heavy boot of Hitler and his armies. There are also attacks on Jews in many areas by anti-Semites who have chosen to follow him.

"Our people are not just having to deal with being spat on and called names, but Jewish children are forced to watch as their mothers cry and their fathers are beaten. Businesses are being vandalized and families are being forced out of their homes into the streets with nowhere to go."

The room is still. David looks at the faces in front of him. He knows he has people's attention but he is aware, because of the importance of this meeting, that he must do more. He continues.

"As we meet here tonight, your Jewish brothers and sisters are being forced into hiding like hunted animals. Many are living in sewers like rats." He pauses, focusing his intense gaze on those standing directly in front of him. "And we will all have to answer for their suffering and loss."

The group is moved by the conviction in his voice. He definitely has their attention.

David stops talking and maneuvers his way through the group. He walks across the room to a table where there is a pitcher of water and glasses, keeping his back to the audience. After a few minutes of what appears to be deep concentration, he picks up the jug and a glass. Seeming to mentally measure the water while pouring it, he fills his glass, pauses, and then begins to drink with slow deliberation. He is using this time to gather his thoughts. What words could he choose that would leave no doubt about the importance of what he is saying?

Refilling the glass with water, he sets it down on the edge of the table, making sure it is separated from the other glasses. He then turns to face the room.

"So here we are—these are the facts as we know them. All of Europe is practically on fire and Hitler makes no secret of his plans for the Jewish people there. But here's the good news. Our resources there tell us that, as far as they know, the Nazis are not stopping any Jew who wants to leave Europe from doing so. They want Europe to be free of all Jews. They say many of the older Jews are already fleeing Europe, even though we've seen only a handful arriving here." He holds up his hand and nods his head. "Yes, I know about the British-enforced White Paper, restricting the number of Jews that can enter Palestine. America and other countries are not too eager to accept and receive Jews either. But we cannot and will not abandon those who are struggling for their very lives, and with God's help we are going to bring them home."

The intensity of his emotions becomes explosive now. He shouts into the room, pounding his clenched fist into the air as if attacking an invisible force.

"We will get our brothers and sisters here by force if necessary! We'll bring them in under the protection of darkness. We'll use boats, large and small—whatever it takes."

He looks through the smoky haze, again focusing on those directly in front of him, his voice hoarse with emotion.

"Do I have to remind you? It's *our* survival that's on the line as well. People! We are at an historical juncture! Future lives are at stake here!"

The room remains quiet. There is a slight shuffling of feet, showing the discomfort in some at the intensity of his words.

David pauses, picks up his glass, and takes another drink of water before returning to the front of the room where he continues to speak.

"I've shared with you the devastating situation and the consequences if we don't get our people out from under the threat of Nazi Germany. Now let me tell you how we plan to do it."

There is another audible shuffling of feet in the room, along with a low murmuring of voices, then silence again. Had he reached them? He couldn't tell. Whether he had reached them or not, it was time to disclose what was going to be asked of them.

"I've told you of the life-threatening situation our brothers and sisters face at the hands of the Nazis in Europe. I am aware of those being helped to leave Europe and of others who are fleeing on their own. I am also aware of the number of young Jewish people who dream of settling here in Palestine one day to raise their families in a place that is safe, a place they can call home. These young people right now are under the threat of Hitler's Nazis and Nazi sympathizers who hate Jews. We have to get them out. You are aware of the crisis we all face here regarding an unknown future of our land in Palestine. This is not something new—you've heard it before."

He hesitates briefly. There is little response from those in the room as they wait to see where this is going. David continues: "We have spent both time and money acquiring large parcels of land from Arab landowners in Palestine. Our people should occupy those lands, where they can build their lives without threat and discrimination. It is inexcusable and utterly irresponsible to let the current situation continue. Our young people, our land, and its resources will all be lost if we don't act now.

"This is our plan. Volunteers, both men and women, will go back to Europe. They will organize the thousands of youngsters who want to come here to join us. There are volunteers there now and they are doing a great job, but we need at least a hundred more. You must understand the importance of all the lives that will be saved, and we have the resources to make it happen. Every one of you is a leader in his or her own right and we need you. I'm asking for your commitment. We need men and women to volunteer who speak German, Yiddish, Hungarian, Polish and Czech. We all know what has to be done. You will not be out there on your own; I give you my word."

The room is still. David knows the decision will be theirs. His tone is relaxed as he concludes.

"I'm handing this to you now—it's yours to accept or reject. Believe me when I say I will respect your decision and I fully understand the weight of what I am asking you to carry. Does anyone have questions?"

These were to be David's final words. His listeners understood the plan. It would involve volunteers willing to leave their homes and loves behind to enter into Nazi-controlled territories, risking their own lives. Their mission: to bring out thousands of Jewish immigrants and transport them safely to Palestine. The future goal for these immigrants was to begin a new life on Jewish-owned land, even though it meant going against the British government who had control of Palestine.

No one had questions. The assembly of men and women collectively thanked David, then remained a while longer, talking among themselves. Aware the British were keeping a close watch on all gatherings by Jews, it was necessary to be discreet when leaving the apartment.

One by one, silently they disappeared into the Tel Aviv night.

The following morning, David met with Zev "Wolf" Ronen to discuss the overall plan needed to enlist as many volunteers as possible from every kibbutz in the region. "Wolf" was a name attached to Zev Ronen by those who knew him within the Central Committee. It was a nickname given fondly and with respect because of his tenacious personality and dogged determination when taking on anything that the organization needed help with. His tall, lean good looks and a thick mane of prematurely silver hair added to the caricature, giving cause for the accepted good-natured teasing within the group. Wolf would go along with their joking, but they all knew that this was where it would end. Once outside of this group he was Zev Ronen. David knew this and could count on him to deliver whatever was needed to get the job done.

First on Zev's list was Kibbutz Yagur. Yagur was just one kibbutz out of many located throughout the region, and like the others it was a tight-knit community. Each member was a partner of the kibbutz, as well as being closely involved in the daily tasks of running it.

The members of Yagur were used to gathering in the great dining hall. Its tables and chairs provided a comfortable place where each day breakfast, lunch, and evening dinners were served. This was a room where stories could be shared about the day's work, along with complaints, much laughter, and—importantly to every member—the hearty delicious food prepared in the kitchen of the kibbutz.

In addition to weekly discussions involving kibbutz business, there was always a lot of good-natured teasing. Everyone looked forward to the membership leader's "gossip of the day" jokes at the beginning of each meeting. The scenario was always the same—with the British often bearing the brunt of Menahem Silver's humor. After one of his jokes, Menahem would pretend to scan the room for people's approval. He would ask the inevitable question: "What do you think? Was it a good one?" The response was always the same—uproarious laughter and moans, with the pretense of suffering, and Menahem pretending to be confused at their rejection. The entire interaction was always lighthearted and entertaining.

Tonight's meeting was to be different. It was well known that visits from the Central Committee only happened when there was something important to discuss. There was more than a little interest in this event, along with a sense of uneasiness among the members because of the British. They could easily consider any large gathering like this to be a threat. Everyone here was aware that the British controlled life in Palestine. Part of that control meant they closely monitored all radio and public announcements, as well as any gatherings they might consider to be political or illegal.

There was also great curiosity among members tonight regarding the reason for such an important figure's arrival here.

One of the men turned to someone sitting next to him: "This must be important."

The other man nodded in agreement. "We'll know soon enough."

The two men took chairs in the back of the room and waited as the other kibbutz members filed in. After a few minutes of exchanging the usual greetings between themselves, the friends and colleagues settled into their seats and a quiet mood descended as they waited.

Sitting beside Menahem was Zev Ronen. Menahem started the meeting with the usual announcements regarding weekly activities and matters concerning the kibbutz. But there were not the usual requests that required a response from members, and the good-natured joking that often accompanied these meetings was noticeably absent. When finished with the announcements Menahem stood up, placed his hands palms down on the table, and said, "That's it."

As Menahem looks around the room at the faces he knows so well, he realizes that what these people are about to hear is going to completely change the lives of some and have a serious effect on all of them. He clears his throat.

"I'm certain that you all either know or have heard of our distinguished guest, so without more words from me, let me offer an introduction." Turning, he grasps Zev's shoulder fondly. "Zev Ronen, I am proud to introduce you to the heart and soul of Yagur—its members."

With this introduction the serious mood is broken. The room erupts into applause and laughter.

Getting to his feet, Zev is noticeably taller than Menahem, who is himself tall. There is an air of confidence about him that is undeniable. The members are still a bit uneasy, but curious to hear what he has to say. Obviously, he has been sent here with a mission that involves them.

Zev makes a sweeping motion with his hand, taking in the entire hall.

"This is something you can be proud of."

The tone of his voice shows genuine pride in the group and sincerity in what he is saying. The tension in the room relaxes. Seeing the smiling faces and heads nodding in agreement, it is obvious to Zev that these people are pleased with what they have heard.

"You are a success," he continues. "Yagur is one of the largest and better-known kibbutz settlements in Palestine. You are blessed."

The group responds in agreement. Zev pauses. He makes direct eye-contact with those in the chairs closest to him; then, with conscious deliberation, he searches out the faces throughout the room. Aware that all eyes are focused on him, he goes on.

"Yes, we are all blessed to be living in this place where we are safe in these times of international turmoil." He raises his hands palms up in a gesture of giving in, shrugging his shoulders. "Oh, I know we're under the rule of the British Crown and we don't have our independence, but this will change one day soon. There is one important thing we must know and that is we are much safer than our brothers and sisters who are living right now, as I speak, under the threat of Hitler and his Nazi regime. The Jewish nation in Europe is in mortal danger. Many of our Jewish sisters and brothers are begging for our help and we hear their pleas to save them. The British are making it hard, but this should not stop us. It is not only our personal duty to help our family members in Europe; it has also become a humanitarian call. We *have* to save them from the Nazis. We must bring them to Palestine and we cannot allow the British to stop us."

His passion is undeniable. He pauses to take a drink of water before continuing. He has to make clear now the reason for his visit and the importance of the burden he is about to place on his listeners.

The group's reaction to what they have heard is quick in coming.

"Damned British!" comes from someone in the back of the room.

Then another voice: "Damned Nazis!"

The room is now filled with voices. Everyone is talking at once. The earlier lighthearted mood in the room is gone.

Zev allows the members to express themselves before motioning that he wants to continue. His own voice is filled with conviction.

"You are right, my friends. Damned British. Damned Nazis.

The Jewish blood of our sisters and brothers is spilling on the streets of Europe as we speak here tonight. It is imperative that we acknowledge the truth: Jews as a people and as a nation are in mortal danger. This is why I'm here tonight."

His tone changes and his voice is low. It's as if he is singling out each member, about to share a secret.

"I'm speaking to you as a group, but I am talking to each one of you personally. I need to enlist your help."

Zev undertsands that the sound of chairs scraping the floor is the result of discomfort. He knows these kibbutz members are questioning what to expect next. He realizes he has to let all of what he has just said sink in.

He waits a full minute, then continues.

"The request tonight comes from the highest level. At this very moment, every member of the Center is meeting with members of kibbutz settlements all over the country. Yagur is one of the largest and strongest settlements. We at the Center are well aware of your willingness to do whatever is asked of you. We are proud of this kibbutz. Some of your sons hold commanding positions in the Haganah, our military branch. Yagur is always mentioned with great honor and as an example of loyal dedication. We knew you would respond in a positive way. You are used to being asked to stand up."

He hesitates again before continuing.

"The need of the hour goes beyond one single kibbutz. We are asking *every* kibbutz to send out volunteers proportional to the number of its members. We need those who speak Yiddish, German, Czech, Polish, and Hungarian. I am asking you to send out at least three men or three women to Europe. I will be leaving to go back but will return in three days to brief those volunteers who step forward. Are there any questions?"

The room is quiet. Zev makes a gesture with his hand, again taking in the entire hall.

"I want to thank you for listening. I appreciate you and the time you have given me. I ask you to think hard about this. It's a serious commitment, one that will not be easy, I know, but I also know the value of the lives you will be saving. Thank you."

Menahem Silver had been listening without looking up from the table in front of him. This was going to be a hard decision to make. He stood up and the two men shook hands.

Zev turned toward the audience once more, said "Good luck," and left the room without ceremony. Menahem watched him leave, then turned his attention to the members.

"We will meet tomorrow for an emergency meeting. You have twenty-four hours. I want each of you to consider and reconsider what has been said here tonight, along with the commitment you will be making. You have a long day tomorrow and you've got some serious thinking to do. Good night."

A few of the members left without saying anything. Others sat in their chairs in silence. After several minutes someone turned out the lights, signaling for everyone to go home.

The next evening, following dinner, members remained in their chairs talking while the dishes and plates of leftover food were being cleared. Shlomo reached for one of the remaining biscuits in front of him.

Benny affectionately tapped on the back of his friend's hand and shook his head, pretending to scowl. "That bread's going to get you, my friend."

Shlomo laughed and stuffed half of the biscuit into his mouth. "You, my friend, are just jealous." Leaning back, he forcefully pushed forward an extended stomach, patting it fondly with both hands, then relaxed. "This stomach is all muscle." He patted it again. "Go ahead—hit it! Come on."

Benny laughed, shaking his head again and turning in his chair. He backed away from the table. "No, you enjoy."

The two men had been friends since childhood, so teasing was nothing new to them.

After everything was cleared from the tables Menahem waited a few minutes, then stood up. A few members continued to talk in low voices. He waited for them to finish their final comments, then cleared his throat as a signal for quiet.

"I want to thank you all for being here again," he began. "I know that your evenings are important and I'm sure most of you are tired after another long day, so thank you. I also want to thank those of you who stepped forward to volunteer for this mission. It's encouraging to know that it is being supported by so many. As a matter of information for you, we have had two more people volunteering from our kibbutz, making a total of five. That's two more than the minimum requested. The additional two will be going later."

Menahem looked down, unfolding the paper on the table in front of him, then continued.

"I'll announce the names of those volunteers who will be leaving first. When I call your name, please come over and join me."

Cheers erupted from the back of the room as he called out the first name: "Shlomo Halperin."

Menahem continued reading from the paper: "Benny Goldberg and Rivka Klein."

There was a loud reaction from the members. They knew this was no decision made lightly. Shouts and the enthusiastic clapping of hands in a show of appreciation accompanied the three as they made their way between tables and chairs to join the director. Menahem shook their hands and hugged each one in a show of warm affection. Turning to the members again, he motioned for silence.

"I would like to thank Benny, Rivka and Shlomo on all our behalf for their willingness to take on this enormously important task. We all know they're an important part of who we are here at Yagur and how much they are needed on the kibbutz."

Loud cheers broke out again—Menahem held up his hands for quiet.

"But we're also aware of our brothers and sisters in Europe who need them more and how their very survival depends on them." He gestured toward the members. "The part you play is also important. Some of you will have to work even harder. You will have to compensate for their absence at the work stations."

He placed a hand on Rivka's shoulder, looking at her with affection. "Rivka, we will miss you and your wonderful cooking, especially your desserts. Shlomo, we will all miss your humor and your music. Knowing how dedicated you have been to the dairy farm, I'm sure the cows will miss you too."

Shlomo grinned and shrugged as a chorus of good-natured moos rang out—from the sad cows where he worked every day.

Menahem continued: "And you, Benny, will be missed, not only by Varda but by everyone in this room." He paused, then looked out at the members and smirked. "Well, maybe not. I'm sure some of these guys who are secretly in love with Varda will be happy to see you gone."

Benny looked around the room and shook his fist, mocking an imaginary threat toward the men in the room. Laughter exploded again.

Menahem allowed the laughter to die down. Then his serious tone returned.

"In a few days you three will be leaving for a training camp, to a location that I am not at liberty to disclose at this time. Shortly afterwards you will leave for Europe. Needless to say, this whole mission thing should not go public in any way." He directed a stern warning toward the members in the room: "Do not mention this when you meet with friends or relatives. This is serious stuff. Do not talk to anyone in Palestine—or anywhere else on this earth for that matter."

With this final warning, Menahem ended the meeting.

2

BENNY AND VARDA

Varda had been listening as the names were announced. She waited in the back of the hall while one by one the members shook hands with Rivka, Shlomo, and Benny, wishing them good luck.

When Menahem announced that Benny would be leaving, it was no surprise to Varda. After getting to know Benny during their six months of courtship, she knew in her heart he was doing what she would expect him to do. He could do nothing less.

There was truth in Menahem's statement about Benny and Varda. She would miss him. There was also some truth when he jokingly said, "Some of the men will be glad to see Benny gone." Varda was considered one of the prettiest girls on the kibbutz. She was strikingly beautiful with her olive skin, long black hair and Mediterranean blue eyes. Along with her beauty, she had a way of seeming to look into the soul of each person she happened to be talking with that made them feel comfortable. More than a few, both men and women, wanted to get to know her beyond the clinic where she worked.

After four years of training as a nurse in Tel Aviv's most prominent medical clinic, Varda had returned to the kibbutz as head nurse and manager of the Yagur emergency clinic. She was part of a medical team led by Dr. Katz, also known within the area as "The Biker Doctor" because of the red motorcycle he rode. As well as being close friends, he and Varda had a long-standing professional relationship. It was not uncommon to see Varda, with her long black hair flying untamed in the wind, on the back of Dr. Katz's motorbike as they traveled between the three clinics located at neighboring kibbutz settlements.

There was always back-and-forth teasing between the single men of the kibbutz about the beautiful Sabra. Varda was well aware of their attention but did not take her would-be suitors seriously. But all of this changed when Benjamin Goldberg, along with a group of newcomers from Europe, arrived in Palestine.

Benny's studies in pharmaceuticals at Prague University, before becoming an architectural engineer, made him a prime candidate for working at the clinic with Dr. Katz and Varda. Menahem introduced him, referring to him simply as "Benny from Czechoslovakia." His dark good looks did not go unnoticed by Varda. Being an independent-minded Sabra, she appreciated his obvious self-confidence. But there was something she couldn't quite understand about him that unnerved her. He had a magnetism she could feel that made her uncomfortable.

As days passed, Varda began looking forward to Benny's time spent at the clinic. She liked watching as he interacted with others. It was obvious how everyone liked and trusted him. But Benny remained somewhat aloof with her. This was not something Varda was used to. Her interest in him became more and more personal.

One evening, as the clinic was closing, Benny stood quietly watching Varda as she was putting supplies away.

"Would you like to join me for dinner tonight in the dining hall?" he asked.

The fact that Benny had been watching Varda made her feel uncomfortable and self-conscious, which was unusual for her. Now this! His question, which seemed to be matter-of-fact, caught her completely off guard, causing her heart to skip a beat with excitement.

He waited as she hesitated, then continued: "I'd feel good about getting to know you better outside of the clinic."

His simple declaration made Varda relax. She was both happy and amused. She tucked her arm under his. "Yes, I'd feel good about that too."

Dinners in the dining hall became regular events for Benny and Varda. They would talk for long periods of time, sharing stories about their past, along with their hopes and goals in a future that for now was unknown. After a while it became common knowledge among members of the kibbutz that Benny and Varda were a serious couple. She introduced Benny to her parents, who were pleased to accept this immigrant as one of the family. Still, among others in the kibbutz, many were wondering about the pair. Where was this romance between the immigrant from Czechoslovakia and their favorite Sabra going?

After the meeting, both Benny and Varda were quiet during the walk back to their small one-bedroom home. Varda remained quiet once inside the apartment. She felt as if the emotions she was experiencing were choking her.

Benny had told her earlier of his decision. He explained that his ability to speak Yiddish, German, Czech and Slovak, as well as knowing the area with its people and their customs, made it his duty to volunteer.

He sat on the edge of the bed, taking off his shoes, and motioned for her to come sit beside him. Reluctantly she agreed, afraid she would burst into tears as soon as she felt his closeness to her.

Benny was silent as he looked down at Varda's hand resting on his knee. Lifting her hand, he placed it over his heart. His voice was soft.

"You are in here and I will carry you every day while we're separated."

Varda laid her head on his chest. She could feel the warmth of his body under his shirt.

He lifted her chin and kissed her. "This will be our first and perhaps our greatest test, my love."

Tonight, they would sleep in each other's arms knowing that tomorrow they would say goodbye.

The next morning, Benny pulled his only suitcase from underneath the bed. He felt a momentary surge of despair. *Here we go again. I thought when I came here this would be home.* He immediately corrected himself. *It is my home.* He dreaded his departure, yet he was aware of the enormity of the mission. He thought about the importance of his task and what it could mean to those he would meet and hopefully save from the threatening Nazi war machine.

He took a deep breath, placed his suitcase on the bed, and began taking his shirts off their hangers in the closet.

Varda was quiet while she helped Benny fold and pack his shirts. Walking over to the dresser, she took his socks from the drawer and slowly closed it. Standing with her back to Benny, she continued to look at the closed drawer. A wave of desperation overcame her. She stood still, holding his socks close to her chest, a feeling of panic suddenly surging through her. She was being forced to let go of this man she loved, not knowing when she would see him again or if she would ever see him again. She could not let him see her anguish. She didn't know how she could hide it, but knew she must.

Benny continued to silently busy himself packing. Once it was finished, there was nothing more to do. He stood in the middle of the room, looking around—this was where they had shared so much of each other. Varda came over to where he was standing. They wrapped their arms around each other in silence. Her face rested against his chest. Benny buried his face in her hair, whispering her name over and over: "Varda, Varda, I love you." Their faces touched in a soft caress. Benny kissed her passionately, as if he were drawing in a life force to sustain him. Varda pulled away, turning her head. She buried her face in his chest so he could not see the tears that would expose all the raw emotions she was feeling. Somehow, she managed the words, "I love you too."

In another effort to gain control and hide what she was feeling, she walked over to the suitcase as if she were going to pick it up.

Benny took the heavy bag from her. "Give that to me, my love."

He set the suitcase by the door and straightened up. Varda tilted her head back and kissed him lightly on the cheek, her face wet with tears. She attempted a small laugh, and her voice was a whisper: "You're going to miss me, you know."

Benny looked down at her. "You know what? You're absolutely right." Taking her by the waist, he picked her up, squeezing her tightly. His own voice was hoarse with emotion. "I'll miss you more than you can ever imagine, my love."

There was nothing left to do now. Leaving the apartment, they closed the door behind them and walked to the dining hall where they would have breakfast together one last time.

3

GOODBYES AND NEW BEGINNINGS

Benny, along with Shlomo and Rivka, would say goodbye to the members of the kibbutz during breakfast. The car was coming to pick up the three volunteers at ten o'clock. The usual lighthearted joking during breakfast had a more serious undertone this morning.

After breakfast the kibbutz members continued with their goodbyes, vigorously shaking hands with the three volunteers, patting them on the back and hugging them with affection and heartfelt gratitude. Each member offered good wishes for a successful mission and safe return. They knew this was a trip into the unknown with certain danger.

The car pulled up in front of the dining hall promptly at ten o'clock. The vehicle was covered in what looked to be remnants of years spent in the Negev. Its driver got out of the car immediately and loaded three suitcases into the trunk. It was somewhat amusing to the members as they watched this man, who looked as if he himself had just walked off the desert, run around the car ceremoniously, opening its doors. His intense behavior, along with his disheveled appearance, was something to capture the imagination of those watching.

After he completed loading the suitcases, the driver stood as if at attention until everyone had said their final goodbyes.

Menahem spoke to those members standing beside him, nodding his head and motioning toward the driver. "That's Noah. He's a strange bird, but a good man."

Menahem had heard all the stories about Noah and his involvement in various clandestine operations. Some he didn't question; others he disregarded as just stories. As for the man's bad manners, they were also well known, shrugged off by some and smiled at by others. In either case, his behavior was blamed on the fact that he was a Sabra.

After Rivka, Shlomo, and Benny were comfortably seated in the back seat, Noah gave a jaunty salute to Menahem and the others. He slammed the car's back doors closed, seated himself behind the wheel, and—without so much as "*Shalom*"—sped off, followed by a cloud of dust.

Once the gate to the kibbutz closed, Noah announced to those in the car that they were on their way to Haifa.

Within a half-hour the car stopped in front of a five-story building that looked as if it housed multiple offices. Almost immediately, two men in business suits approached the vehicle. They unloaded the suitcases from the trunk, then nodded and smiled at the people inside the car.

Noah turned to his passengers in the back seat.

"This is it," he announced. "*Shalom* and *mazel tov*."

As soon as they stepped out of the car Noah sped off again, leaving them in a cloud of dust. The three were amused. They looked at one another and grinned. But they didn't have time to give him much thought. They were instructed by the two men in business suits to bring the suitcases and follow them into the building.

They walked down a long corridor before taking a freight elevator that stopped at the fifth floor. Here they got off and were ushered into a large room where they were told to wait.

They could observe the room from where they were standing just inside the door. It had been set up to accommodate meetings. Chairs were arranged in rows facing a long, banquet-style table. Two large schoolroom blackboards leaned against the wall behind the table, one with a detailed map of Europe attached.

It wasn't long before two other men, also in suits, appeared, acknowledged them briefly with smiles, picked up their suitcases, then disappeared through an adjoining door. Benny motioned to chairs, and the three of them sat down to wait for the unknown to happen.

In a matter of minutes, the adjoining door opened again. A woman entered, carrying a tray with three small cups of what looked to be Turkish coffee. They thanked her and turned down her offer to bring them food. They watched as she disappeared once more through the same door she had entered. The coffee turned out to be Turkish as they had guessed.

The two men who had accompanied them from the car returned before they had finished drinking the coffee, bringing with them two more volunteers. The small group introduced themselves. The two new arrivals were from Geva, a kibbutz located just 30 kilometers east of Yagur. The older-looking of the two introduced himself as Moshe. The younger man, who looked to be in his late twenties or early thirties, told them his name was Yossi.

It wasn't possible for everyone to introduce themselves to those already in the room before the next volunteers arrived. New arrivals acknowledged others with a nod or a smile before sitting. Some took the initiative to talk briefly with those close by, while others seemed preoccupied with their own thoughts, keeping to themselves while they waited.

The process of bringing in volunteers continued until Benny calculated the group's total to be twenty-three.

After a short time, the side door opened again. This time they recognized Zev Ronen, accompanied by a tall woman with dark hair. The two seated themselves at the table in front of the room and continued their conversation, ignoring the group in front of them. The woman lit a cigarette, inhaled deeply, then turned and focused her attention on the group of volunteers. Her expression was serious as if she were studying each face. Without looking away from the group, she nodded her head as if in agreement with something Zev Ronen had said.

Propping an elbow on the table, while resting her chin on a closed fist, the woman took another drag on her cigarette. She released the smoke slowly, continuing to stare at the faces in front of her.

Finally, Zev pushed his chair back and stood up, addressing the volunteers.

"I'm certain that some of you are familiar with Zelda, but for those of you who are not, let me introduce you. This is Zelda Levinson."

Zelda lifted her hand, acknowledging the introduction. She gave a casual wave to the group, without relinquishing her cigarette.

At the recognition of her name, reaction was instantaneous. Just being in the room with Zelda Levinson was considered to be an honor. Her courage, as well as sharp tongue, was legendary. The stories about Zelda Levinson's fearless ability to stand up for her beliefs were well known throughout Palestine. She was recognized as being the voice for every Jew.

Zev waited to allow the excitement in the room to settle. He shook his head and laughed: "I knew you'd like her."

He waited again for the applause to subside before he became serious.

"Zelda will be speaking to you in a few minutes, but first I have some things I want to lay out for you."

There was no stirring in chairs or turning of heads now. All attention was on Zev.

"You have taken upon yourselves a serious responsibility," he began. "Everyone at the Center shares in this with you, without exception or reservations."

He continued. "You are going to spend a week or so together in directives and training sessions. Your instructors, for the most part, are members of their own active teams. They have been in the field but have been instructed to come back here to train you so that you'll be able to join their teams and eventually start up new teams of your own. Even as we speak here tonight, there are several other locations where more volunteers such as yourselves are being trained. Each one of those groups will depart to its assigned destination when their training has been completed, and you will do the same."

The room was still as everyone took in the enormity of what he was sharing and what it meant.

Zev went on: "There will be no time off or leaves during this time and going forward. You will not be meeting with your loved ones anymore."

These words came together in Benny's head along with thoughts of Varda. His stomach lurched for a fleeting moment; then just as quickly, the feeling left, as he continued listening.

"You have until tomorrow morning to reconsider," Zev stated, "and this is critical, not only for you and your loved ones, but for the project and those very lives that will be depending on you." He looked around the room. "If anyone present in this room feels that he or she has taken upon themselves something they may find too much to accomplish, please decide now; no one will think less of you. You can return home tomorrow with our gratitude for coming here, along with our blessings."

He turned and motioned to Zelda, who had been taking in everything he said, along with the reactions from the volunteers.

"Now I would like to invite Zelda, who came here today from Tel Aviv, to say a few words." He laughed. "She's much better-looking than I am and even I get tired of hearing myself talk."

Zev walked back to his chair. His words had lightened the mood again. He took a long drink of water and nodded to Zelda, who immediately crushed out her freshly lit cigarette in an ashtray in front of her and stood up.

"Well, that's the only compliment I've received today," she quipped, "and I think I'm going to accept it. Thanks."

Zelda's Speech

The attention was focused on Zelda now as she walked around to the front of the table. She took a minute to clear her throat, then spoke with a clear voice.

"I am personally so proud of each and every one of you. Believe me, if I was young and had half as much energy as you, my children, I would not be sitting or standing here at this table. I would be sitting in one of those chairs among you. I would like nothing more than to go with you and take an active part in your mission." She turned toward Zev, smiling. "But I guess someone has to stay back home and take care of the old farts at the Center."

She put her hand on Zev's shoulder and smiled again, affectionately. "Excluding you, my darling."

Everyone laughed, including Zev. Zelda cleared her throat again before continuing.

"You all know the time is short and there is much to be done." Her voice had a serious tone now. "The British are being pressured to become more aggressive and limit the number of Jews permitted into Palestine. They will allow only a few hundred a month. Europe will soon become a deathtrap for millions of Jews. We cannot possibly accept such a scenario. As long as it's possible, we need to rescue, not a hundred people a month, but thousands—and this is where you come in. We need to bring our brothers and sisters out. Naturally, the young ones who have no responsibilities are able to leave for their own safety, but each and every one is important, young and old alike. You will be going from town to town, from village to village. You will bring out everyone who wants to make a move to Eretz Israel. There is no time to waste. You have already heard the facts about what is going on there. That's why you have volunteered; I don't have to repeat them. I cannot impress on you sufficiently the importance of your mission. You have our gratitude, as well as the future gratitude of those souls whom you will rescue and may never meet."

With those final words Zelda kissed her hand and offered it as a wave.

"Thank you, my beautiful children."

Making a mock salute, she turned from the group to rejoin Zev. The two of them waved their goodbyes to the room and left through the same door they had entered by.

Zev Ronen's offer to reconsider the mission was not something

33

Benny would accept. He knew that he would miss Varda—being separated from her would be tough. But this, and what he was to become a part of, was too important to give up.

Not long after Zev and Zelda left, another woman, accompanied by four men, entered the room through the same side door. They seated themselves in chairs behind the long table. After a short while, one of the men pushed his chair back and stood up. He was good-looking, tall and well-built, with thick, curly black hair. Benny guessed him to be in his early thirties. There was no discernable accent that Benny could detect as he began to speak.

"My name is Nahum," the man began, "and that should be sufficient for now. You will get to know all of us as we proceed, but, for security reasons, please understand there will be no last names. We are your instructors. In other words, we are going to teach you how to become separated from who you are now, as you sit here, and who you will be when we are finished."

Those words alone commanded everyone's attention.

He continued: "Secrecy is critical. We prefer that you limit your outings to a minimum—and, for your information, there is no available budget for eating out."

While Nahum was talking, one of the other men got to his feet. He waited a minute, then spoke without introducing himself.

"I understand that each one present here is fluent in Yiddish and Czech, and some of you speak German, as well as Hungarian and Greek. If this is not the case, let one of us know after the meeting. This group is going to Czechoslovakia, pretty much to the area of Slovakia where most of you came from.

"We will begin speaking in Yiddish, Czech, and Slovak to refresh your memories. I'm sure you haven't used these languages for a long time, because the majority of you have been living in kibbutz communities for several years, away from Europe."

Benny guessed that the one speaking now was Slovakian-born. The logic for speaking Yiddish was clear to the group of volunteers because of the areas they would be going into. It would definitely seem strange to them, however. Since arriving in Eretz Israel they had been encouraged to speak the ancient Hebrew language. They were also encouraged to use Hebrew first names. Now they would be required to go back to speaking Yiddish.

Some of the volunteers found the entire thing amusing. The thought of speaking Yiddish brought back loving memories of parents, of aunts and uncles. It would be almost like going back in time. Yiddish was their childhood language and an important part of their way of life. It was also one they had decided to leave behind to immigrate to the Land of Israel. The volunteers realized that in a few weeks they would be meeting people on a daily basis who spoke nothing but Yiddish.

The group seated at the table continued taking turns, speaking to the volunteers. They went over in great detail what could be, and would be, expected of everyone in the coming weeks and months. It was comforting for some of those listening to know this assignment was going to be temporary.

Training and Orders

The next few days were filled with intensive training. There were specific classes for men and women. The volunteers were divided into small groups of four and five. The members of each individual group were to memorize the names and locations of specific cities and villages. Some of the names were unfamiliar because they were new.

Both men and women were required to go through physical training classes, along with various self-defense tactics, known as Krav Maga. The only means of self-defense for the volunteers would be the ability to use their hands and feet, along with other parts of their bodies, as combat tools. They were taught to be ready at all times for every possible situation. Later, they would be training others to use the same defense tactics. Pistols of any kind would not be allowed, under any circumstances.

Travel documents were handed out. The time for departure was coming closer each day. Those volunteers who had arrived in Palestine legally were told to use their passports and documents. Those who were in Palestine illegally were given forged documents, produced by the clandestine department of the Haganah, which was the military arm of the Center. A detailed travel plan was created for each member of the group. They were furnished with tickets and cash, partly in the form of local currency, partly in the currency of their destinations.

Volunteers were to leave the area individually or in pairs to avoid drawing attention to themselves from the British authorities. Air travel was available only to the British, so it would be necessary to use the more common means of transportation, such as ships, trains, and buses. Each member of the group was given addresses and meeting points along the way to Europe, such as in Greece, Romania, and Turkey. They would be disguised as tourists, traveling in small groups of three or four, until reaching their final destination. Experts who were familiar with the territory had carefully planned out every detail. Nothing had been left to chance.

It was time to say goodbye to Rivka. She was to leave with a different group. Benny was to board a Greek vessel, carrying both goods and passengers. Shlomo would board the same ship. They both received information about the ship they would be traveling on, but their orders were to ignore each other until reaching the Port of Piraeus in Athens. The vessel was able to accommodate a maximum of forty passengers. They also received a warning about the possibility of British spies being on board.

Leaving Haifa Port

The military checkpoint was situated at the main gate of Haifa's port. Benny appeared to be calm, but he was tense as he approached the neatly uniformed officer stationed behind a green metal table.

The officer checked Benny's Palestinian passport, flipping through its pages carefully. After a few minutes he stamped the ticket, handing it back with a smile: "Thank you—have a safe trip."

Benny took in a deep breath and exhaled slowly. He had been concerned about the checkpoint, having been forewarned about possible extensive questioning that could take hours. He considered himself lucky as he walked to where the ship was moored. He could relax now.

The *Christina* was old and showed signs of serious wear. Rust had replaced the paint long ago, leaving her name barely visible. Benny joined the group of passengers who had arrived earlier. They were told to wait until the loading of all barrels and merchandise was completed.

The port was a hub of activity. Trucks and cranes were moving heavy crates and barrels into position so they could be loaded onto the cargo ship. Loud orders were being shouted back and forth from the pier, between Jewish and Arab port-workers and Greek sailors aboard the ship, creating a mixed discord of all three languages—a noisy cacophony. Benny remained beside his suitcase on the pier, watching the activity that surrounded him with amusement. He saw Shlomo dragging his suitcase toward the group that was waiting; his friend glanced briefly in his direction, then ignored him.

After the loading was finally completed and all trucks had left the pier, an order was given for passengers to embark. Everyone picked up their suitcases and walked up the steep ramp to board the ship. They were welcomed by a uniformed crew-member. Each passenger was given a piece of paper with a cabin number on it, along with a second piece of paper with a corresponding number that was to be attached to their suitcase. They were told a member of the crew would be bringing the suitcases to the cabins later.

When Benny found his cabin, he was pleasantly surprised to discover it was situated on an upper deck and not deep inside the ship, as he had suspected it might be. Inside the cabin there was one small bed, and a small bathroom with a shower. He was going to have the place to himself.

Before long there was a knock on the door. A young Greek sailor dragged the heavy suitcase into the room and placed it on the bed without saying a word. After the sailor had left, Benny stepped out onto the deck. He leaned against the ship's railing, taking in the panoramic view. The city of Haifa was built on a gentle slope of Mount Carmel. The sight of it, with its white buildings covering the mountain as far as the eye could see, filled Benny with emotion. He imagined briefly what it would be like if Varda was with him to share in the beauty of it all.

Two loud blasts of the ship's horn brought him back to the present. The ramp was raised and, almost simultaneously, the ship started moving. After reaching a safe distance from the concrete pier, the *Christina* edged slowly forward as the small tugboat began towing her out of the harbor. Benny felt a surge of loneliness as they left the Haifa port, heading out into the open sea.

The Mediterranean Sea was not new to Benny. He remained on the deck for a long time, leaning over the ship's railing. The calm beauty of the water was relaxing to him. He thought about

Varda again and the friends he had left behind at the kibbutz. He remembered when he had made the last voyage to Palestine. It was less than three years ago that he had arrived in Haifa on a British passenger ship. Times were different then. The rumors of Germany building its military and the threats of war would have seemed unreal a few years ago. This trip for Benny would be different. He was taking a trip into the unknown.

More than an hour passed. The sea was becoming rough. Benny's hands gripped the railing. He looked down into the rolling waves as they disappeared beneath the ship's hull, causing a slight up-and-down motion. He thought about those passengers below who might be getting seasick. Three years earlier when he was on his way to Haifa, the British liner was caught in a storm off the tip of the Italian "boot." There had been many green faces—lots of retching and throwing up among the passengers. It was not fun for those affected. He remembered standing on the deck, watching the huge waves. Thinking about those below now, he said aloud, "Thankfully, this isn't going to be a storm."

Turning away from the railing, he returned to his cabin.

During the days that followed, obeying the instructions given by his trainers in Haifa, Benny didn't initiate any contact with other passengers. Occasionally he and Shlomo exchanged glances while eating in the ship's dining room, but they continued to avoid any sign of recognition.

Benny had a lot of time to think. Again and again his mind returned to Varda and the clinic. He also thought about his parents, whom he hadn't seen since going to Palestine. He wondered if he would be able to meet up with his family while in Prague. They had no idea he was coming to Czechoslovakia and he could not tell them about the mission.

4

ARRIVING IN GREECE

After five days they arrived in Piraeus. It was a busy port. The *Christina* waited almost two hours before the crew could tie her up to the pier. The passengers lost no time offloading themselves, along with their luggage, and heading to a spot where taxis were lined up along the pier, hoping to pick up fares. After being cleared by passport control officers, they would be able to leave the area.

Benny waved to the nearest available taxi. Its driver jumped out, greeting Benny with a friendly smile from under a very large gray mustache. After lifting the suitcase with ease, he loaded it into the trunk of the taxi and opened the door, directing Benny into the back seat: "Get in. Where do you want to go?"

Benny acknowledged the driver's greeting with a nod. "Hotel Acropolis."

On the way, the driver was more than a little talkative, chatting about his family, his political views, and the weather. Benny found himself smiling back at the mustached face in the mirror, paying little attention to the unending chatter while they sped through the streets of Piraeus. He grasped the door handle tightly, bracing himself against what he considered to be an accident waiting to happen.

When they arrived at Hotel Acropolis the driver swung into a parking space and slammed on the brakes, causing Benny to grab onto the back of the seat in front of him.

Benny laughed. "Well, you're quite the driver!"

Getting out of the cab, he shook the driver's hand and paid him. He was relieved the ride was over.

"Thanks for getting us here."

The driver grinned. "Any time. I'm at your service."

The man handed Benny a small piece of paper, then got back into the taxi and drove off.

An amused Benny smiled to himself, shaking his head. He looked down at the crumpled paper in his hand; it had a name and number on it. He smiled again. "Nice to meet you, Christo." He put the paper into his pocket.

Benny entered the lobby of the hotel and set his bag down in front of the desk. The clerk welcomed him but said very little while handing him a key.

"The bellboy will bring the suitcase to your room. You're on the third floor."

Even though hungry, Benny decided he would wait to get something to eat until after seeing his room. The rest of the day and evening was his to do with as he pleased. Tomorrow the group leader would contact him regarding the trip by train to Slovakia.

The next day, Benny received a telephone call from someone who introduced himself only as "the group leader in Athens." There was no polite exchange during the call. The caller did not give his name. He directed Benny to attend a meeting being held at a private residence belonging to a "Joseph Alkalay" and gave him the address. Benny had heard the name mentioned before but couldn't recall when, how, or where.

Walking out of the lobby onto the street in front of the hotel, Benny waved to the first of several taxis that were waiting to pick up passengers. He opened the door of the taxi and got into the back seat. The driver turned to smile. His mustache was unmistakable.

Benny gripped the driver's arm in a friendly gesture.

"Hello, Christo. It looks like we're going to become friends while I'm here." He patted the driver's arm. "But do me a favor and take it easy. You took ten years off my life the last time."

Christo laughed as he pulled away from the curb, turning his taxi into the street. "Good to see you again, my friend. I'll take it easy. For me it is nothing. I guess for you, it is something." He laughed again, turning his attention to the traffic that was heavy this time of day.

Benny relaxed, letting his body sink into the seat's worn cushion. He enjoyed Christo's humor, along with his heavy Greek accent.

True to his word, Christo kept the speed within acceptable limits while making conversation. He told Benny about local restaurants that offered the best Greek food, and gave him advice regarding other points of interest throughout the city.

A half-hour later the taxi stopped in front of the address that Benny had been given. Christo handed a business card over the back of the seat.

"I know I gave you my name before, but here, take this—it's my private telephone number. If you need a ride to anywhere, call me. I'll take you anywhere you want to go."

Benny thanked him and took the card, putting it into his jacket pocket. He would keep this card.

Christo waved goodbye and sped off, with tires screeching.

Benny stood for a minute, taking in the heavy iron gate and six-foot-high wall, covered with vines. Behind it was a short drive leading up to a sprawling two-story brick house. There was a young man standing in front of the iron gate who had obviously been waiting for the taxi to leave. He opened the gate for Benny.

"*Shalom.*" Speaking in Hebrew, he told Benny that he was waiting for three more people to arrive, and directed him toward the house.

Benny took hold of the heavily carved brass door-ring and knocked, then waited. Another young man who looked to Benny to be in his twenties opened the door. Like the other man at the gate he spoke Hebrew, and asked Benny to go into the living room. He advised him: "When everyone has arrived, we'll get started."

As soon as Benny entered the large living area, he spotted one of the men from the meeting in Haifa sitting on a couch across the room. He was engaged in conversation with another man Benny didn't recognize. This man was well tanned with thick gray hair, dressed in a gray pinstriped business suit. The two men stopped talking just long enough to look over and smile, acknowledging his presence. Benny nodded and smiled back, then looked around the room. He recognized all the members from his group, along with Shlomo.

Shlomo left those he was talking to and walked across the room to where Benny was standing. Slapping Benny on the back, he gripped his friend's hand. "Good to see you, my friend."

Benny gripped Shlomo's shoulder, then hugged him. "Good to see you too. I'm really glad you're here. Finally, we can speak."

The two men hadn't been assigned to any specific city in Czechoslovakia. Benny hoped he and Shlomo would be sharing the same team or location, because he knew they could always rely on each other.

The young man from the gated entrance appeared now with a woman and two other men. He motioned them toward chairs, then walked over to speak to another man whom Benny remembered seeing in Haifa. He was curious about who this man from Haifa was, but recalled instructions given during training about "no name or first name only."

In a few minutes, someone unknown to Benny got to his feet and cleared his throat as a signal for those in the room to stop talking. He began by welcoming them: "*Shalom.*"

The group responded in the same way: "*Shalom.*"

The man continued speaking in Hebrew.

"Before the meeting, I want to introduce all of you to Joseph Alkalay, who has so generously offered the use of his beautiful home for this important gathering."

The man in the gray pinstriped business suit stood up. He smiled at the group, giving a slight bow, then sat down again. Everyone applauded to show appreciation for his generosity, then waited to hear what was coming next. They were certain the reason for this meeting was about to become known.

The one speaking was brief and to the point.

"This entire group, including myself, will leave early tomorrow morning by train. We have reserved a section of sleeping carriages. There will be a few stops and train changes. We will be going from Athens, heading to Macedonia. At Skopje we will switch to another train that will take us to Belgrade in Yugoslavia. This train will then continue to Budapest. In Hungary we are going to do another switch to a train that will take us to Bratislava. This will be our final destination. Each one of you will receive the train tickets after this meeting.

"During the trip, which will probably take three days, I will give you the name of the Bratislava hotel where we will meet with local representatives. They are anxiously waiting our arrival. You will have plenty of cash to buy food on the journey. There is a restaurant on every train and, from my personal experience and previous trips, I can tell you that the food is pretty good."

Benny raised his eyebrows and nodded at Shlomo, who shrugged back at him. Who was he? The speaker had left nothing to guesswork, except who he was.

Now the man's focus was once again on Joseph Alkalay.

"Talking about food, there is a delicious Greek buffet waiting for us in the dining room, prepared by Mrs. Alkalay. But before we go in, Mr. Alkalay would like to say a few words to the group. For your information—and this is important—Athens is flooded with British agents and informers. I don't have to tell you that our presence here must be kept a secret. Now let's hear what Joseph has to say."

Joseph Alkalay stood up.

"As you may know," he began, "a good part of my family already lives in Eretz Israel. But unfortunately, not many members of the Jewish community here in Greece share the views of my family. They believe Palestine is not a place for them. Many say Hitler will never come to Greece. They are too busy with their lives and have businesses here.

"However, I would like to tell you, on behalf of my family, that we admire and support your mission with a warm heart. God bless you, and God bless those you will be saving.

"Now let's go in and eat, shall we?"

One by one, each member shook Joseph's hand, thanking him for his hospitality, before going into the dining room where the buffet was being served.

The man who had spoken earlier was becoming more and more of a curiosity to Benny. It was obvious that this person held a highly secure position within the membership group. There was also the probability that he would be in charge during the entire mission. Not knowing even his name was unacceptable to Benny. He made the decision to change the situation in spite of what the rules had been in Haifa during training.

After filling his plate, Benny walked over to where the man was standing and extended his free hand in greeting. "This is a wonderful gathering you've set up with the Alkalays," he began. "It's much appreciated."

The two men shook hands, smiling at each other.

Benny continued: "Since we're going to be traveling together, I regret we haven't been introduced. My name is Benjamin Goldberg. My friends call me Benny."

The man took a bite from a piece of bread that was on his plate.

"I'm Daniel. I appreciate your taking the initiative to correct the lack of introduction. It was an unfortunate oversight on my part—one I have to apologize for." He looked thoughtful, continuing to chew for a minute, then smiled. "Being so involved with details, I overlook some things."

Daniel took another bite of food from his plate and nodded toward Benny's plate. "This is really good Greek food, isn't it." It was more of a statement than a question.

Benny, tasting some of the soutzoukakia from his own plate, agreed. "If this is an example, I'd say Mrs. Alakay has prepared a Greek feast. I'm going to check out the spanakopita." He extended his hand again. "It's a pleasure to meet you, Daniel. I'll see you in the morning. Enjoy the buffet."

Benny walked over to where Shlomo was reloading his plate. He put his hand over Shlomo's plate as if to protect it, laughing. "Save some for me, my friend!"

Joseph Alkalay joined an amused Daniel, who was watching the interaction between Shlomo and Benny.

Daniel motioned in their direction. "It took a lot of *chutzpah* for Benny to approach me. I'm sure he knew I purposely did not introduce myself. I had him figured right. He is exactly what is needed."

Leaving Athens: The Long Train Ride

The Athens train station was busy with arriving and departing passengers at seven in the morning. Daniel was speaking with each member as they arrived to make certain they were prepared for the long journey. He methodically went over his list of members' names, checking them off after reviewing the tickets they had been given the night before. As soon as they were approved, each member hurriedly boarded the train. Thanks to Joseph Alkalay, they would be traveling first class with assigned seats.

As soon as all members were on the train, Daniel boarded to join them.

At 7:30 sharp, the train began to move out of the station. The two black locomotives spewed dense white clouds of steam as they gained speed, traveling toward the suburbs of the sprawling city. Passengers could hear the loud warning whistle announcing its impending arrival before every intersection. Within 30 minutes the train had passed through the city limits and was hurtling along at full speed.

Benny walked over to a window, pulling it up so he could lean out. He liked experiencing the wind's force against his face and upper body. The Greek countryside, with its olive groves, vineyards, and farmed fields, passed by quickly. Occasionally a herd of sheep or goats became visible, but rapidly disappeared into the distance.

Benny thought of Varda and tried to imagine what she might be doing. Thinking of Varda reawakened the raw hurt of having to leave her, making him sad. He forced himself back to the present, watching as the countryside began to change. Soon the train would be making its stops at cities and small towns. Closing the window, he returned to his seat.

It was a first train experience through Greece for many of the volunteers. The beauty of the countryside captured them as it passed. The only one unimpressed with the view was Daniel. He had made this trip several times before. He preferred reading a book to seeing what had become so familiar to him.

As the train reached mountainous terrain, it slowed. Its engines had to work hard to pull the loaded carriages into the rolling hills.

Those who had been at the windows of the train returned to their seats. It had begun to get dark. Some of the group decided they were hungry and walked to the restaurant carriage for dinner.

They were still within the borders of Greece when total darkness fell. Those who had gone to the restaurant carriage for dinner returned. Daniel asked the conductor to show them to the sleeping carriage, directing the men to separate quarters from the women. Each sleeper compartment was the same and was outfitted comfortably with two bunks.

It didn't take long for each person to appreciate their bed. The constant motion of the train and the sound of the engines made it hard for some to fall asleep, but eventually the long day took its toll and by midnight most were sleeping soundly.

Macedonia

By the time everyone awoke the next morning to look out the windows, the train had made its way into the countryside of Macedonia, where it would continue making frequent stops at small towns and villages along what was destined to be a monotonous route.

Being confined together on the train was a good way for the members of the group to get to know one another. Some were becoming better acquainted because they were eating meals together. Others made no attempt to socialize beyond a friendly greeting, before retreating back into their own space. This was accepted without question.

When the train arrived at Skopje, the capital of Macedonia, it was already dark. The group would be changing trains here, which meant they had to collect their luggage and get off to wait for the next leg of their journey.

When the designated train finally arrived, it was close to midnight again, which meant the volunteers had been standing on the station platform for more than three hours. They would be grateful when their suitcases were loaded on and they could start moving again. This train would continue now toward Belgrade in Yugoslavia.

As soon as the suitcases were taken care of, the group made its way to the restaurant carriage for a late dinner, then to the sleeper carriages. The noise and movement of the train would not bother them tonight. Tonight they would sleep.

Entering Yugoslavia

The next morning, they found themselves crossing the border of Yugoslavia. The conductors checking tickets were accompanied by uniformed police officers who were asking to see passports. It was a tense moment since some of the documents had been produced by the Center.

The officers suspiciously scrutinized every passport, along with the face of each passenger. Upon inspection, all the documents appeared to be genuine and were reluctantly returned to their owners without questions or comment.

The next two days went by smoothly and without incident, although the train ride was becoming increasingly tiring because of its frequent stops. Once deep into the countryside, members welcomed its ever-changing beauty.

Benny and Shlomo spent time together, talking about the upcoming mission. They also reminisced fondly over Kibbutz Yagur and its daily routines, which now seemed so far away. At one point Benny closed his eyes as if to sleep and thought of his last night with Varda. He wondered when he would see her again.

Entering Hungary

It wasn't long after the train passed into Hungarian territory that there was another passport inspection. This time the Hungarian police were doing the inspection. After all documents were inspected and considered to be in order, they were returned to their owners with a smile and a polite nod of recognition.

It was already late afternoon when the train pulled into Budapest's central station, where the group would change trains once more. The train that was to take them to Bratislava, Slovakia, was already waiting to board on the platform opposite to where they were offloading. They grabbed their suitcases as soon as they were set down and hurried across the platform. The train started leaving the terminal almost before they were settled in their seats.

Bratislava was to be their final destination. They forgot how tired they were. This long train ride was going to end in a few hours. They were en route to Bratislava, a familiar territory to many of the members, who spoke the language and were familiar with the city.

5

THE MISSION BEGINS

Arriving in Bratislava

The train arrived in Bratislava early the next morning. As the volunteers departed the train, they were greeted by a group of half a dozen younger people, all welcoming them with hugs and handshakes.

A large bus was parked by the station's boarding platform. Its Slovakian driver smiled: "Good morning."

Another six young people were excitedly waiting as the group members climbed onto the bus. The driver waited until everyone was seated before starting the engine. He would take them to the small town of Osik, to a camp located outside of town.

Some members among the youth group began to sing. The volunteers grinned to one another as the youthful voices sang chorus after chorus of Yiddish songs. These were some of the young people they were here to bring home.

Benny glanced at Shlomo, who was seated next to him. He tilted his head to the side. "Do you hear those voices? This is what it's all about, my friend. They're a big part of our mission."

Shlomo nodded his head in agreement. "Now we begin."

When they arrived, the driver, with the help of some of the camp's residents, offloaded the luggage into the entrance of the main building. The travelers were pleasantly surprised to see Rivka, who had arrived at Osik earlier. She directed everyone into the dining hall. Benny spoke briefly with her, then left the group to look for Baruch, who was the manager of Camp Osik. He would meet with him before leaving for Bushtina the next day.

Bushtina: Meeting Wolf Schneider

The train station in Bushtina was small, consisting of a single platform and a small brick building with a ticket office and a waiting room kept clean by the ticket agent.

It was almost dark when Benny stepped off the train with his suitcase. This was the last train of the day and there were few passengers. A horse-drawn carriage was parked alongside the station platform. In the driver's seat was a tall bearded man, who Benny guessed to be in his fifties. Baruch had given Benny a description of the man who would be picking him up. The description fit.

Benny approached the carriage, speaking in Yiddish: "Are you Wolf Schneider?"

The man got down from his seat, smiling, and extended his hand toward Benny. "Yes, I'm the one. Who told you about me? Reb Yeed, my Jewish friend?"

Benny shook the man's hand. "Baruch Goldfarb from the Osik village camp told me good things about you."

Wolf picked up the suitcase and put it on the floor of the carriage.

"We haven't seen Baruch in such a long time," he mused. "We

were wondering what had happened to him. We thought he'd returned to Palestine. He used to stay with us, in our home, during his many visits to the area. Such a nice fellow. Are you also with the kibbutz?"

"Yes, I'm associated with the kibbutz," Benny replied.

Wolf was happy to meet a fellow Jew who spoke Yiddish. He asked Benny to sit beside him.

"I would like you to stay with my family if you don't mind," Wolf offered. "There is only one small inn here. There might not be a vacancy tonight. We can try tomorrow if you want, but my private inn has the best prices in Bushtina—it's free."

They both laughed.

Benny accepted Wolf's offer. "Of course, it will be an honor to be your guest."

The two men continued talking as they drove to Wolf's home. It was an easy conversation, one that included Wolf telling Benny about a talk he had had two weeks earlier. The local policeman had told him about all that was going on with Nazi Germany and the threat to Jews.

Benny told him that he, along with others, had been sent from Palestine to Europe. He described the alarming political situation for Jews under the Hitler regime, and gave details of how the living environment was becoming more and more intolerable for Jewish people—in what was once their home country. He continued: "It's important that all of you must leave and come to Palestine, where you'll be safe."

Wolf's voice was low and thoughtful as if talking to himself. "I agree. Something must be done."

When they arrived, the two men went into the house. Wolf introduced Benny to his wife, Rachel, then went back outside, where he unhooked the carriage and took the horse into the barn to be fed and watered.

Once the horse was settled for the night, he returned to the house. Benny was already seated at the dinner table and was engaged in conversation with Rachel, along with their two daughters and a son. They had introduced themselves while waiting for Wolf to return.

There were many questions for Benny during dinner. He answered in great detail, giving them as much time as they needed to get to know him and his reason for being here. Wolf expressed his concerns for the welfare and safety of his children if they moved to Palestine—due to the growing tensions between the Arab and Jewish populations, as well as the British control over the entire territory. Benny was careful not to minimize the difficulties of the situation in Palestine. At the same time, he had to point out his honest views on the grave future developing for all Jews in Europe.

Wolf's daughters asked questions about the kibbutz way of life in Osik. Benny told them that he was a member of Kibbutz Yagur in Palestine, going into great detail about life in that community. The girls were particularly interested in hearing about the lifestyle of the kibbutz and showed their excitement over the prospect of making many new friends. Their brother Menahem, who was the oldest of the children, remained quiet and noncommittal. Wolf announced that his son and his girlfriend, Gittel, were planning a wedding within a year and her parents would not want her to leave home before getting married.

The dinner had taken hours. Before they realized, it was past midnight. Wolf showed Benny the guest room. It was a small but welcoming room.

Benny lay on the bed, going over tonight's details. He genuinely liked Wolf and Rachel. He turned his head into the pillow, pulling the quilt up to his chin. *What a loving family*, he mused. *I wonder how many families I will meet like them?* He fell asleep very quickly.

Wolf and Rachel lay in bed talking. They were happy about the prospect of saving their children from the Nazi threat. Their prayers had been answered, but their hearts were heavy. They said good night and, holding each other's hand, went to sleep.

The next morning over breakfast, details were worked out between Benny and Wolf. With his knowledge of the area, Wolf would be Benny's carriage driver for ten days. His personal relationship with those who were as concerned as he was for the future lives of their families would be important. Benny's goal was to reach young people to be introduced to the camp in Osik, where they would become trained in skills that would prepare them for being a part of kibbutz life in Palestine. It would be important for him to enlist encouragement from the parents of those young people who were old enough and wanted to leave home. These were to become the young pioneers who would secure a future for those who would follow.

As soon as Benny received a commitment from twenty or thirty youths, along with their parents, he would take the train back to Osik to make the necessary arrangements. He would return to Bushtina with train tickets, along with another volunteer who could help him bring everyone safely back to the camp.

Dora and Sarah started to plan their trip as soon as Wolf and Benny left the house. They ran to their bedroom and began pulling coats, dresses and shoes out of the closet, excited at the thought of leaving, along with the prospect of having a new life and making new friends. Dresses and coats soon covered the beds, along with personal items, and shoes were scattered on the floor.

But just as quickly as they had started, the girls stopped. "We don't have a suitcase!" they cried. "What are we going to do?"

They both sat on the bed between the piles of clothing, staring at the empty closet.

"We've never been anywhere. We've never needed a suitcase before."

They had never considered leaving their village before this. The realization that they actually would be doing something, going somewhere, was exciting, but it also created a problem.

Sarah picked a shoe off the floor and looked helpless. "What are we going to do?" she repeated.

Dora thought for a minute. "Maybe we can ask Yankel Katz— maybe he has a suitcase. He travels outside the village sometimes."

Sarah continued to look at the shoe in her hand. Turning it over, she studied a worn spot on the sole.

"No, that won't work. He probably has only one suitcase and we need one for each of us." She looked at the pile of clothing on the beds. "Look at everything we have!"

Dora stood up and walked toward the door, ending the conversation. "Well, we'll just have to tell Father to talk to Benny. He'll figure it out."

She left the room with Sarah following.

Wolf and Benny returned late, tired but feeling good about their day. Immediately upon arriving, they were confronted by a somber son and two stressed daughters.

Both girls started talking at once: "We can't leave! We have no suitcases!"

Benny sensed their frustration and knew he needed to come up with a quick solution for them. He would sort the whole thing out later.

He grinned at the two of them. "Well, now that's a problem. I can't see you carrying all of your belongings over your shoulders, so I'll have to bring you back some suitcases. How many do you think you'll need?"

The girls were pleased at how easy he made it all sound. They felt a bit foolish for their panic.

"Well, one for each of us will be great."

Benny smiled. "Good! Consider it done."

Wolf had been observing the entire scene. He had never seen his two girls so upset. They were usually so unemotional. He realized this must be very important to them.

Rachel had dinner on the table, so any more discussion with the girls would have to wait.

As they ate, Menahem announced that Gittel's parents would not give permission for her to leave for Palestine until they were married. He had tried to convince them, but they would not change their minds. The young couple would just have to wait. Menahem was disappointed but would not leave without Gittel.

Benny reassured him by telling him that he would be returning in ten days from Osik, and in the meantime the parents might change their minds. He offered to meet with them.

Menahem thought it would be worth trying, but said he would talk to Gittel first. The two left it at that.

Wolf and Rachel lay in bed talking deep into the night, until Rachel finally kissed him on the cheek and said good night.

Wolf continued to lie in the darkness, thinking. Seeing his two daughters so upset over the possibility of not being able to leave, and his son disappointed over having to wait until later, when he and Gittel were married, made him even more aware of how important it was for his children to have a better life.

59

Wolf was used to his life with Rachel in this small mountain village, nestled at the base of the Carpathian Mountains. It was home. He never took its beauty for granted. The forest with its beautiful rivers and the spectacular mountain peaks could be harsh in the winter. But the family accepted the cold and snow. His carriage would become a sled for hauling passengers and supplies to and from Bushtina during the winter months. Theirs was a hard life. When Rachel became diabetic, needing insulin shots daily, they accepted that too. This was the life he and Rachel were born into.

Wolf didn't blame his children for wanting something better, especially with the threat of Nazi Germany. But he and Rachel would be heartbroken to see the girls leave, and taking care of the small farm without them would add hardship to his wife, who already worked too hard for her condition. All of these thoughts weighed heavily on Wolf's mind as he lay in the darkness. And there was one thought he couldn't ignore: They might never see their children again. Tears slid down his cheeks as he lay there. He was glad that Rachel couldn't see them in the darkness.

The next morning Benny left with Wolf. They would be traveling from village to village, meeting with Jewish families.

In every location, they talked with them about Hitler's plans to expand beyond the borders of Germany, vowing to liberate Czech citizens from all Jews. Benny shared word from Munich of Hitler's plan to annex the Sudetenland for Germany and how it could mean war between the two countries. It was hard for the parents to learn of Hitler's goal to eliminate Jews, not only in Germany but also wherever Germany would rule. Occasionally Benny's words were met with skepticism and negative reactions from mothers and fathers. The young people, however, all liked the idea of leaving the villages for a better life, accepting with open minds Benny's plan for a more promising future in Eretz Israel. They were excited about the thought of working on a kibbutz and joining other young people in a pioneer movement to build a new life.

After ten days of driving from village to village, meeting with parents and young people, Benny had made mutual commitments between himself and over three dozen young men and women. These past ten days, luckily, were without trouble or incident.

Wolf drove Benny to the train station. He would miss his new friend. He enjoyed sharing stories with Benny about passengers he'd met. Some of his stories about their behavior sounded so outrageous Benny couldn't help but laugh, which made Wolf laugh too, remembering them. He also liked hearing of Benny's life on the kibbutz and his love for Varda. He could understand Benny's loneliness, as well as his commitment to a mission that was becoming critical for the lives of so many. This had been an adventure for him.

It was to be a short trip back to Osik for Benny. He planned on meeting with Haim, the volunteer who was to oversee the safety of those traveling by train from Bushtina to Osik.

Having them feel secure was important to him. He had made this a priority when choosing the volunteer who would be traveling with them. Most of these young people had never been away from home before. Benny was aware that even in the excitement of what was to be a new adventure for them, they were nevertheless saying goodbye to their families.

There were a few other things to take care of, such as acquiring suitcases for Dora and Sarah.

Benny would be returning from Osik in seven days. These seven days would allow everyone to prepare for what was going to be a long trip. They would be embarking with others on a journey into the unknown.

Seven days later Benny walked out of the train station carrying a large suitcase and accompanied by a young man in his twenties, wearing a leather jacket and boots, who was also carrying an oversized suitcase. Without hesitation they headed for Wolf's horse-drawn carriage, which was parked just beyond the station platform.

Wolf jumped down from the driver's seat and slapped Benny on the back affectionately. "Welcome back! You're right on schedule." He nodded recognition toward the other man, smiling "Welcome."

Benny introduced Haim to Wolf, explaining that Haim would be traveling with the group back to Osik. After Wolf helped put the suitcases into the back of the carriage, they climbed in and headed toward Wolf's home.

When they arrived at the house, Menahem, Sarah and Dora were waiting for them outside. As soon as the two girls saw the suitcases, they ran to Benny and hugged him. He laughed at their uninhibited show of appreciation.

Haim stood back, observing the welcome Benny was receiving. He grinned at Wolf.

"I didn't know suitcases could cause so much excitement."

Wolf shook his head and smiled at Haim. "These girls have been waiting for Benny and those suitcases all week."

Once in the house, Rachel offered the three men freshly baked rugelachs, along with hot tea, which they accepted gratefully.

Menahem informed Benny that he had not been able to convince Gittel's parents to give their permission for them to leave before the marriage. So Menahem and Gittel would not be traveling with them to Osik. Benny was concerned for the young couple but said no more about it. He only hoped they would be safe.

Talk about travel plans continued. Most of those who had signed up to leave for Osik would be at the station tomorrow. They would take the afternoon train, accompanied by Haim. Benny would stay another day in case some of those who were committed did not show up at the station. He wanted to make certain everyone had the times and date right. This was all new to these young people, so there could be some confusion.

Benny agreed to Dora and Sarah's request to wait another day and travel with him instead of going with Haim and the group. Wolf hadn't thought of it but was relieved, knowing they would be in good hands. Their departure was going to be hard on Rachel. Maybe the girls leaving with Benny would help.

Early next morning the three men left for the train station. Haim and Benny would wait at the station while Wolf drove his horse-drawn carriage to the outskirts of Bushtina and the surrounding villages. He would pick up the families and drive them to the station. After the parents had said goodbye to their children, he would take them home again.

He gave his horse the signal to go. It was going to be a long, hard day for everyone, including the horse. He was glad his own children wouldn't be leaving until the next day so that he could spend time with them tonight.

Transporting passengers from the villages to the station, Wolf couldn't help overhearing the tearful last-minute advice given to the children by their mothers in the back of the carriage, while the fathers sat in stiff silence on the seat next to him. Because he was a father, he understood that he would have to remind himself to remain strong the next day and not show his emotions.

Benny checked off the list of passengers booked to be leaving. There were seven young people who were not at the station. He would check on them tomorrow, but for now it was important to see this group board the train. Wolf agreed. He still had to take those parents home who had come to say goodbye.

The train arrived on schedule and offloaded its passengers. It was time now for Haim and the anxious group of twenty-nine young men and women to board the train. It was also time for goodbyes. There were hugs from mothers not wanting to let go of their babies, now young adults, leaving for the unknown. Fathers were shaking hands with their sons, now young men, setting off on an adventure that they wouldn't share. There were sobs from those mothers, and tears running down the cheeks of otherwise strong men, as they watched the train being boarded. The dream of a future with the children of their youth was being taken from them, leaving them standing on the platform, waving as the train began slowly moving away from the station. This was to be their final goodbye.

6

ARRIVING IN OSIK

Hours later the train pulled into the station at Osik.

A truck with a flat open-carriage bed and side slats was waiting in front of the station platform. Haim laughed good-naturedly as he patted the side of the truck.

He introduced himself to the driver. "You're not hauling hay today, my friend."

The driver nodded, smiling. "I know! I've made this trip before. Glad to have you here."

Haim shook his hand through the open window. "We'll have you loaded up in a few minutes."

It took a while before everyone was off the train with their suitcases and ready to load. There was laughter and excitement as the youngsters climbed onto the flatbed and crowded together for what was going to be a long ride to the camp. After they were all on board, Haim climbed into the front of the truck with the driver. He could relax now. He wondered how Benny was making out.

It was late when Benny and Wolf returned home. They talked for a while, drinking tea and eating the small sandwiches Rachel had made for them. The girls told them they had already packed and were ready for the trip. Menahem was quiet, not saying anything. He sat glumly listening as his sisters chattered with excitement. Wolf knew Menahem was disappointed, but it had been the young man's own decision not to go against Gittel's parents. Wolf was secretly relieved that he would have one of his children remaining home—because of Rachel's diabetic condition.

When Dora and Sarah came out of their bedroom in the morning, their father had already left with Benny to collect those who had missed their train the day before. Rachel and Menahem said very little at breakfast. Both girls were torn between their eagerness and excitement to get to the train station, and concern for their mother. They couldn't help but notice their mother's appearance. Rachel's face was pale, covered with red blotches, her eyes swollen from crying. Dora handed her a damp cloth from the kitchen and told her to lie on the couch, which she did, obeying her daughter weakly. She continued to rest without speaking until Wolf arrived hours later to pick them up for the ride to the station.

As soon as he saw Rachel lying on the couch in such a weakened condition, he became alarmed. He pulled a chair over so he could be close to his wife. His voice was gentle as if talking with a child.

"How do you feel? Do you want me to ask the girls to stay?" He was afraid his wife might not be able to endure the departure of her daughters.

Rachel looked up at him. Her eyes were filled with tears and her voice was hoarse.

"No, no, they must leave. I'll be better tomorrow." She grasped his hand in hers and managed a smile on her pale face. "Don't you worry too much. I'll be stronger tomorrow. I'm stronger than you think."

He kissed her affectionately on her cheek. "I know, I know." He had to remain calm for her sake.

Wolf grabbed the heavy suitcases. "Menahem, look after your mother."

Dora and Sarah each kissed their mother. "Goodbye, Mother."

They kissed Menahem on the cheek and hurriedly left to take their places in the carriage. As soon as they were seated, their father headed for the train station.

When they arrived, Wolf hitched the horse and accompanied his daughters to the station platform. A pleased Benny was standing with yesterday's missing young men and women, along with their family members, waiting for the train, which was just arriving now. Its arrival gave no time for long goodbyes between Wolf and his two daughters.

Benny and his group, including Dora and Sarah, hurriedly boarded the train. Wolf was left standing on the platform with the other family members. The two girls leaned out of the train's window as it moved slowly away from the station. They could see their father was crying as he waved his white handkerchief in a final goodbye.

The train with Benny and Shlomo, along with their group, arrived early the next morning in Osik. They were met by a group of enthusiastic members from the kibbutz training camp who helped them carry their luggage to a bus parked outside the station.

The driver welcomed them warmly before starting the engine. Once the bus started moving, a few of the young people began to sing. Before long the joyful noise grew louder as others joined in, continuing to sing in chorus until the bus was filled with their voices as they traveled toward the kibbutz.

Benny and Shlomo, sitting in adjoining seats, turned toward

each other and smiled. The ride in this old bus on a dusty road through the countryside had become a celebration. It seemed to Benny that the ones who were singing off-tune were making up for it by singing more loudly. He put his hand on Shlomo's shoulder.

"These are just a few of the young people we are here to bring home."

Shlomo laughed. "We're going to enjoy the journey, my friend."

Both men leaned their heads back against the seats. Benny closed his eyes, smiling to himself. His body relaxed back into the seat of the bus as he listened to the singing. Keeping his eyes closed, he allowed his mind to replay the last weeks. *This is what it's all about*, he thought. *The meetings, the planning, the long train rides, and leaving Varda.* He took a deep breath and exhaled again, releasing all the tension he had been feeling since leaving Haifa.

When they arrived at the camp, Benny directed the group to the dining hall so they could get something to eat, even though it was late. He would meet with Baruch later. It had been a long day, but now they were here and they would be hungry.

Many camp members were still sitting around the hall, talking. Benny motioned to the empty tables.

"Let's eat! Tonight, we'll take what we can get." He laughed. "And if you're as hungry as I am, it will be exactly what we wanted."

Two of the dining-room staff brought them plates of cold salad with dinner rolls and slices of chicken, along with glasses of juice.

They began eating at once. Benny was right: it was "just what they wanted."

After they finished eating, the members wanted to meet one another. Introductions began with yesterday's arrivals and tonight's newcomers who had arrived with Benny and Shlomo. Finally, everyone agreed it was time to get some rest. Shlomo would be leaving again tomorrow morning early, so he said goodnight to Benny and went to his room.

The members of the new group were shown rooms where their suitcases were waiting. Dora and Sarah would be sharing a room with two other young women, one of whom was already asleep. The other introduced herself as "Betty, Haim's younger sister." She showed them their closet spaces, then led them to the common bathrooms and showers.

Looking directly at both girls, Betty made no apology for the cramped accommodation. "There are many of us here now and we must get used to living in crowded conditions. It's not easy but it can be fun. It depends on how you look at it."

They liked Betty. Pulling their pajamas out of the stuffed suitcases, the two girls got into bed. They covered themselves with thick woolen blankets and went immediately to sleep. It had been a long and emotional day.

Dora was the first of the sisters to wake up. The other girls had already left to go to the dining hall. She called to Sarah but got no response, which was not unusual—Sarah was used to sleeping in at home while everyone went about their daily routines. The family all knew that waking her up before she was ready could set off a firestorm of her anger. Sarah had a temper that most times was hidden by her sweet disposition. Dora had never risked an outburst from her sister, but being here at the camp was different from being at home. Sarah would have to learn.

This was to be the beginning of Sarah's private training. Dora mustered up her determination to teach her sister a lesson in personal responsibility and anger control. She took a deep breath and reached for the covers that Sarah had pulled over her head.

"Come on, Sarah, it's time."

Sarah's reaction was immediate. Looking up from her pillow, she turned over to face her sister. "Leave me alone! Who do you think you are?"

Dora continued to pull on the covers while Sarah resisted, clutching them with both hands. Dora now gave a forceful tug, freeing the blankets from Sarah's grasp.

Her sister reacted angrily. "No! I'm tired—go to hell—leave me alone!"

Dora reached down, grabbing her sister, and attempted to roll her out of bed. Stumbling off balance, the two girls ended up slithering onto the floor.

Dora got to her knees. Lifting one leg over Sarah, she sat on her stomach to hold her down.

"Listen to me!" she said firmly. "Your temper tantrums aren't going to work here. You wanted to join all this, so now you're going to join in and stop being a brat. If you can't grow up and be part of it, I'm going to ask Benny to send you home."

Sarah's body relaxed under her sister's weight. She began to cry.

"Let me up, Dora. I'm just tired, that's all. Of course I want to be part of this."

Dora got to her feet. "Good, now let's get ready and go for breakfast. I don't know about you but I'm starving. There's a management meeting this morning with Baruch right after breakfast. I think it's important not to miss it."

She took her sister's hand and helped her to stand.

The two girls walked into the dining hall and hurriedly sat down at one of the available spaces. Sarah smiled sweetly at the young woman who served them, thanking her. She was back to being herself again.

They ate quickly because the tables were being cleared and the meeting was about to begin.

Introduction to Life in a Kibbutz

After the tables were cleared, Baruch stood up.

"I want to welcome all of you newcomers to our camp," he began. "You have now become full partners in a unique and outstanding organization.

"You are part of a community of young pioneers on the road that will take you to Palestine. This camp is only the beginning. Your training here will prepare you for future kibbutz life. Some of you will help to form a new kibbutz in Palestine; others will join an existing kibbutz, depending on circumstances."

He continued: "This is a training camp. You will work at various jobs and learn occupations that will be useful for your future life in Palestine. Some of you will work outside of the camp. Your earned salaries will become part of a common cashbox. You will receive your full board, along with petty cash for expenses, based on availability and individual needs. This is how every kibbutz operates."

It was important that every new member understand the workings of a kibbutz, as well as the rules of this camp and what they could expect. An important part of the volunteer messenger's job was to have gone over with the recruits and their families what Baruch was talking about now, so this was not going to be a surprise to his listeners. He would still need to assure them of being able to leave and return home if they didn't think they could adjust to this way of life

The group were listening closely as he continued: "Should any one of you think you can't adjust to this life and want to return home, we will make sure that you receive all you need for a safe journey back to your families."

There was no response. Baruch waited a few moments, then continued the meeting by introducing some of the other members who would be in contact with the newcomers. He called up Saul, the bookkeeper, who would be handling their pay envelopes and all personal expenses for them. Next, he introduced Haim as the one who arranged all job placements for outside the camp and work schedules for inside the camp. Some newcomers knew Haim from traveling with him on the train from Bushtina. During the train trip a couple of the girls had developed a crush on him and fantasized about getting to know him better at camp. Haim stood up and introduced his wife, Leah, to the group as the dining-room manager. It was obvious that some of the girls were disappointed to find out that he was married.

Leah got to her feet. She was still wearing an apron over khaki-colored shorts and shirt with her hair pulled back into a ponytail. She smiled at the group.

"Hello," she said cheerfully. "I'm sure we'll all get to know one another and I look forward to working with some of you."

She sat down again, taking the chair next to her husband. This would be the end of any crushes on Haim for these girls, but there would be others, based on the ratio between young men and young women in the camp.

Meeting Jacob

Baruch smiled toward the young man sitting next to him, motioning for him to stand.

"This is Jacob Friedman," he announced. "Jacob is the farm and garden manager."

Baruch placed his hand firmly on the young man's shoulder, giving it a squeeze. "Jacob came to us when he was a teenager—a skinny teenager, I might add." Laughing, Baruch slapped Jacob on the back. "Look at him now."

Jacob was visibly embarrassed as Baruch continued praising

him, pointing out that he had recently graduated from agricultural school and was an excellent gardener. It was obvious that Baruch was fond of, as well as proud of, this young man.

Dora felt some of Jacob's discomfort. She could understand Jacob's shyness, as she herself never liked to be focused on. She always hated it when her father complimented her to his friends for her cooking or said how pretty she was.

She couldn't help noticing Jacob's deep tan. He had obviously acquired it from being out in the fields. She was a bit critical, but in the end she decided that because of his thick black hair and tanned, muscular body he was quite good-looking, in spite of his somewhat long and pointed nose. She thought maybe they should get to know each other better.

After the meeting was over, along with the introductions, Haim got to his feet and announced that there was to be another meeting. This time the young people would meet with him in Baruch's office. Because of the size of the office, they would be separated into smaller groups or would meet individually, depending on their job or work schedule.

During the time spent in Osik, the girls would take turns with household chores and laundry, along with training in gardening and caring for small farm-animals such as chickens, geese and ducks. They would also be assigned to kitchen duties. Learning to cook would not be difficult, since most had cooked under the guidance of their mothers at home. The training would prepare them for life on a kibbutz when they reached Palestine.

The young men would begin at once to learn carpentry and fieldwork. An important part of the training for everyone was to include teamwork and loyalty to one another.

Jacob left Baruch's office after the last meeting and went up to his room. He was glad to have some time to himself. His work clothes were still soaking in the sink, waiting to be washed. He would need to wear them tomorrow.

Despite his tiredness, Jacob washed his shirt and pants and draped them over the makeshift clothes line he had created—using two chairs he had spaced apart and tying a heavy cord to the back of each chair. Taking a jacket from the wardrobe, he placed it under the pants and shirt, which were still dripping small amounts of water, even after wringing them out. He reasoned it wouldn't do to let them make the floor wet, and he could always hang the wet jacket up to dry while he was at work tomorrow.

The room that had always seemed so welcoming to Jacob seemed cold and barren to him now as he lay on the small bed. He let his eyes wander around, taking in the two wooden chairs that had become a drying rack for his clothes. He concentrated for a few minutes on the wet clothes and dripping water that was making its way, one drop at a time, to land silently on the jacket below. He studied the beautifully hand-carved wood on the doors of the wardrobe against the wall; he couldn't help thinking that somehow it seemed out of place in the room. Jacob turned his head to one side on the pillow, glancing at the small table that held a lamp beside his bed, then returned his focus to the ceiling.

For the first time, because of Baruch's introduction, Jacob could feel the pain of the loneliness that had been with him since leaving home as a child. Tears ran silently down his cheeks. He could taste the salt they left, allowing them to dry without wiping them away. His chest felt heavy from the sadness he felt, as he fell asleep, without undressing.

As Jacob slept, visions of black rushing water swirled around him, as he struggled . . . Other visions of tiny grasping hands, reaching out for one another in the darkness, caused his heart to pound against his chest, waking him. Soaked with perspiration, he forced himself to return to reality.

Jacob recalled the flood that had ravaged their village and the events leading up to it. It had rained relentlessly for over a week. The dam, further upstream, had failed and collapsed from the heavy rain. The entire village, which was built in a valley, was overcome by a wall of muddy, rushing waters.

His family had just finished their evening meal when they heard the unfamiliar sound. Within minutes, and without warning, the water had flooded the house, carrying with it bags of feed and farming tools from the yard outside. Everyone was swept off the chairs they were sitting on. The table and chairs, along with furniture being carried in from other rooms, moved about ominously in the swirling flood, threatening the small children as they reached out for help in the sudden darkness.

Jacob's mind replayed the scene of them escaping the rising water by groping their way up the flimsy stairs into the attic. The cries as they huddled together in that cold attic remained vivid in his mind. He remembered his father's stern orders to "stop crying." And his mother's quiet reassurance, telling them "Everything will be all right." He recalled how he fell asleep holding his sister, her small hands holding onto him tightly, making certain she was safe in his arms.

The water eventually receded, leaving behind its destruction, along with a thick layer of mud on the floor. The family cow was gone, along with most of the chickens. The river returned to its banks, and the village was left to return to its life in the valley, but it would never be the same.

His mother died shortly after the flood. The reason for her death was never talked about. Jacob wondered if this beautiful, gentle woman with her quiet strength, whom he loved so much, just got tired. Now Jacob shook his head as if to clear it of these memories. He lay there until finally falling asleep.

It was beginning to be daylight and Jacob had to get ready to go down to the dining hall, eat, and go to work. He took his dried shirt and pants from the line and replaced them with the now wet jacket. He got dressed slowly and left the room, closing the door behind him.

Looking down the hallway at the closed doors that lined it, he took a deep breath and exhaled, thinking, *It's going to be a good day.*

Jacob and Dora

After breakfast Jacob met with the girls to go over their work schedules in the fields. During the meeting with Dora, she made it clear she would prefer to work outside the kitchen if possible. He appreciated her assertiveness but told her he had nothing to do with her schedule in the kitchen and dining room; she would be expected to share time inside, working in the dining room and kitchen with the other girls.

Dora thanked Jacob and left. She was satisfied she would only have to work part-time in the kitchen, which she hated to even think about, and part-time in the garden and fields. Maybe, working with Jacob, she would get to know him better. She liked that idea.

Work in the gardens and fields was tedious. Ongoing weeding required constant squatting and bending, as the workers made their way up and down the rows. There were sore muscles in the beginning, making cool showers at the end of each day before dinner important to the girls.

Dora had made friends with Betty, one of the young women she shared a room with. She confided her secret attraction for Jacob, making Betty a willing co-conspirator in her getting to know him better. Since Betty was a hostess in the dining room, she could make sure Jacob would be seated next to Dora whenever possible.

Dora watched the interaction between Jacob and others in the fields, as well as in the dining hall. He took management of the camp's farm very seriously. She liked his sense of humor, which surfaced when he was talking with the other members at the table. It was obvious he was liked and respected.

The ease of the relationship between the two of them was growing, but Jacob still showed no attempt to go beyond his interaction with Dora in the dining hall. Outside, he paid little attention to her. When speaking to the workers as a group, he seemed to purposely ignore her. Frustrated, Dora wondered, *What do I have to do?* She answered her own question: *Nothing, I guess.*

One afternoon several days later, Jacob stepped into the field unannounced. He was in a lighthearted mood. He complimented everyone again on the good work, not addressing anyone in particular. Dora was watching him closely as he spoke, taking in his rugged good looks. She imagined what it would be like to have him just come over to her!

Now he was about to leave, after talking with one of the workers. Her heart sank. *What's wrong with him?* she asked herself. *Does he just hate me? He talks to me in the dining hall—why not here?* Frustration was about to bring her to tears.

Jacob said goodbye to the others, then glanced over to where Dora was standing and nodded in her direction, grinned, and winked. Overwhelmed, she almost stumbled over the basket of weeds in front of her.

Later, in her room, Dora lay on the bed, allowing her feelings to take her to a place she had never been before. Her thoughts were interrupted as the other girls came in. It was time to go down for dinner. Her mind was whirling with excitement: *Will I see him there? How should I act? I can't tell my roommates. I probably can't even eat.*

But she didn't have to worry about her roommates. They were busy sharing their own day's events with one another. Her secret love for Jacob was safe for now.

The arrival of new members in the camp had noticeably ceased. The names of those scheduled to depart for Palestine were posted on a board in the dining hall and checked daily. There were also disturbing rumors in the camp of rabid anti-Semitism spreading throughout the area.

In the meantime, the days of learning and long hours with hard work continued. Jacob's mood had changed to one that was more lighthearted. He was still serious about his duties as farm manager, but Baruch could see a difference in how he reacted to others, especially Dora. He smiled to himself. Could Jacob be in love?

Strong bonds were being formed between members of the camp. Jacob and Dora's friendship began growing more serious. It eventually became an accepted fact to everyone that they had become a couple.

Jacob's work-hours were getting longer. Jobs were willingly shared to make up for the vacancies created by those who had left for Palestine. Everyone was waiting anxiously for their name to be on the departure board.

It was almost dark when Jacob left the gardens. Once inside the dining hall, there would be a lot of the good-natured chatter that went with dinner. He thought it would be good to relax for a while alone before going in.

Sitting down on the grass beside the road, Jacob looked toward the farm buildings and beyond to the fields. The thought came to him: *I will be able to see this exact view one day in Palestine.* He felt excitement well up inside him as he envisioned the future for everyone here at the camp.

Letting his mind wander, Jacob remembered the day when he first arrived at Osik. The memory of being lost and hungry, walking seven miles from the Osik train depot in the dark with a backpack, remained fresh in his mind, even now. It was not the first time he had become lost, finding his own way. At six years old, tragedy had struck in his life, setting Jacob on a path that was very different from the happy childhood he had shared with his family. They had lived in the small village of Brusturi, located in the Carpathian Mountains of Slovakia. Jacob had blocked the dark memory, but the other night, asleep in his room, it had surfaced and he had set it free.

Sitting here now, surrounded by quiet, he could remember his sisters and brothers playing with other children from the village along the banks of the fast-running river. He remembered the excitement of waiting for the dam to be opened, an event that would allow thousands of pine logs into the rushing stream of water. They would use a long pole with a metal hook on one end to capture logs that had broken loose from their piles as they floated close to the shore while being transported down the rushing river. It was considered to be a hunting expedition. Jacob remembered how proud they were of their bounty. The timber would become dried firewood for cooking and heating their homes during the winter months. Little did he know at the time how this same river, providing exciting games of sport, would take from him with a vengeance.

Being one of ten children, left with a father who was broken in spirit and grieving after the flood, Jacob was separated from his sisters and brothers. He was sent to live with relatives, along with any family willing to take him into their home. He would have to pack up and move from family to family as often as three or four times a week, getting used to sharing a bed, clothing and food. He would hear of his sisters on occasion, but would never see them again.

Later on, an older brother heard of a movement for young people wanting to go to Palestine, and joined a camp in Osik for training. He found Jacob and gave him a train ticket to the same place, along with directions, telling him, "Use these for a better life." His brother was among those who had already left for Palestine.

Directions to the camp had been confusing. Jacob had had nothing to eat since the previous day when he finally arrived, tired and thirsty. He remembered taking a deep breath and ringing the bell on the gate. A young man opened the gate and Jacob recalled his almost frantic introduction: "I am Jacob Friedman. My brother, Eliezer, told me that you are looking for young pioneers. So here I am."

Looking down at the ground now, remembering, Jacob shook his head thinking, *That was not an introduction. It was a desperate cry for help. Where was I? I didn't know. What was my future? I didn't know. What I did know was that it was night, I was hungry and thirsty, and I was tired.*

He had become a part of a new family very quickly. He still missed his life as that small boy with curls, who studied the Torah and played alongside his sisters and brothers, under the loving care of a mother and a father. Sitting here now, he made a promise to that little boy: *Never will I abandon you or the memory of you.* He made another promise, this one to the man he had become: *Never will I forget who I am.*

Jacob pulled a few blades of grass from the ground where he was sitting. Holding them to his nose, he inhaled deeply. The fresh smell brought him back to the present. Reluctantly he got to his feet, thinking, *It's going to be a busy day tomorrow.* He took another deep breath, inhaling the smells of the camp that surrounded him. He said aloud, "And it's going to be a good one."

He headed inside to get cleaned up for dinner.

Dora was happy to see Jacob enter the dining room. She quickly walked over to him. He smiled down at her and without any embarrassment took her face between his hands and kissed her.

Baruch grinned. *I knew it. Jacob is in love.*

The Meeting

The purpose of Benny and Baruch's meeting was to discuss plans that had been headed up by a Jewish businessman, Berthold Storfer, and the Nazi Adolf Eichmann. Eichmann had been given the assignment by Hitler to get rid of all Jews from Europe. Storfer was a well-known figure among Jewish circles in Vienna with known social contacts with Eichmann. Even though he had a questionable character in the views of some Europeans, the delegation in Europe made the decision to allow him to help save Jews, because lives depended on him. His handling of monies to be dispersed and arrangements for safe travel was critical to the success of the mission. Baruch and Benny agreed; working with Storfer was a risk that had to be taken.

The following morning after their meeting, Benny left the camp to go into the surrounding villages. Shlomo, along with the other volunteers, had left earlier and had not returned.

Weeks passed. Daily life in the camp continued, but it had changed.

There were no new names on the departure board. There were no new arrivals and no one was leaving Osik. Dora had written to her parents earlier to tell them about Jacob, but wasn't sure they had received her letter because mail was no longer being picked up and delivered. There was much concern among the young members. It was as if the camp was suddenly isolated.

Benny Returns with Frightening News

Finally, after being gone for weeks, Benny returned. As soon as he arrived, he scheduled another meeting with Baruch in his office.

Closing the door behind him, he wasted no time. He sat down in the chair opposite Baruch's desk, keeping his voice low so that only Baruch could hear what he had to say.

"The Nazis have taken over Czechoslovakia," Benny announced. "Hungary has allied itself with Germany, and with Germany's help has taken control of the Carpathian region of Slovakia. Every aspect of daily life has changed. There is fear and confusion in the streets. Slovakia and Moravia have fallen, and parts of Russia have been taken over. Eichmann has the ear of Hitler and has made an agreement to allow Jews to leave. Eichmann wants all Jews to be relocated at once to Prague, and the situation worsens each day. We have to get these people out of here."

Baruch leaned forward across his desk so he was closer to Benny. "There were government officials here just yesterday," he said quietly. "They told me they were with the new Slovak government and wanted a list of everyone living at the camp. They also want reports of any changes in the future. I'm glad you're here. We have to close down the camp. I'm instructing the management of the young pioneers that everyone will be relocated to Prague. Jacob will be in charge of dismantling the farm. We'll sell what we can—and give the rest to Carl Taller, who has been a close friend and supporter of the camp."

Benny agreed. "We'll have to move everyone out in smaller groups so they won't be noticed; their safety is critical. We will all remain in Prague for a few weeks until our departure for Palestine has been arranged. I'll get the tickets and make all the arrangements. Shlomo and the others will be arriving about the same time in Prague."

Baruch took a deep breath and walked out from behind the desk. "Well, we've got our work to do, so let's do it."

The two men shook hands. Benny grasped Baruch's arm. "We will, my friend. We will."

Benny left the office and Baruch went to find Jacob.

Closing Camp Osik

Closing the camp went smoothly under the supervision of Jacob, along with the cooperation of the young pioneers. They were excited about leaving. This was what they had been waiting for. Their dreams of a future in Palestine were about to become a reality.

When Jacob told Dora that they would have to be separated until later, when they would meet in Prague, she was not happy. He tried to explain to her that it was necessary for her safety. He told her they had to leave and travel in small groups, and he would be going later when he finished his responsibilities at the camp.

But his explanation didn't make sense to her. She was used to her stubborn optimism being able to overcome any obstacle. Her tears frustrated Jacob now, since he knew there was nothing he could do to reassure her. He felt helpless and wasn't used to feeling helpless. Before, he had only himself to take care of, but now he felt responsible for Dora's feelings. Walking away from her toward the barn was hard, as a sobbing Dora returned to the main building. He didn't look back.

Later, Jacob returned to look for Dora. When he found her, he saw her face was red and swollen from crying. He pulled her gently to him.

"Surely it can't be that bad," he said. "We'll only be separated for a few days." He stroked her hair lovingly. "Come on now, you're a big girl. You can handle a few days without me, can't you?"

He tried to cheer her up by teasing her. But she pulled away, looking up at him with tear-filled eyes.

"You don't understand, Jacob. I was going to tell you tonight after dinner—I'm going to have a baby. We are going to have a baby."

Jacob stopped breathing for a minute, then recovered his composure. Taking her face between his two hands, he looked into her tear-filled eyes. "Are you sure?"

Dora backed away from him. Now she was angry. "Of course I'm sure, and now we're leaving the camp and we don't know when we'll even see each other again."

She started crying again. Jacob reached for her, pulling her back into his arms.

"Don't worry," he said. "It will be all right. When we reach Prague, I'll find a rabbi and we'll get married."

Baruch had told Jacob that they would only be in Prague for a short time. Everyone would be going on to Bratislava. They would board river-going boats in Bratislava that would take them to a port on the Black Sea, where they would embark on ships that would take them to Palestine.

Jacob reassured Dora that everything would be as Baruch had told him. Holding her, he cradled her close to him. "Just think, my love—our child will be born in Palestine."

Dora rubbed her face against Jacob's shirt. He kissed the top of her head lovingly. At the same time, he was wondering what the future held for them and their baby.

7

ARRIVAL IN PRAGUE

The move from Osik to Prague went smoothly. Each group as it arrived was met at the train station. The groups were to be broken into smaller groups of ten or twenty and transferred to separate locations across the city where they would be housed in small inns. One larger group was to be housed in a hotel that could accommodate fifty people.

Benny told Dora that he had arranged with Baruch for Jacob to join her at the hotel. When she heard this good news, Dora threw herself against Benny with such force that she knocked him off balance. Stumbling backwards, he regained his footing and returned her hug.

He laughed. "Well, Jacob told me you're about to get married, so we couldn't have it any other way."

He advised her to wait with the others at the hotel until Jacob arrived. Then he left to find Baruch; they would need to make certain that all went as previously planned.

Shlomo met with the other group leaders to make sure everyone had their allowances for food. They would have to eat in town at local eateries and be aware of their surroundings at all times. Each group was given directions on keeping a low profile because the city was under German control.

Within a short time, everyone was checked in and Shlomo returned to the hotel and met up with Baruch and Benny. The three men went to a local restaurant, where they had bratwurst and a shared pitcher of beer. With everyone in place now, they could relax to some extent. However, they couldn't let their guard down completely during these next few weeks, because Prague was under Nazi control. So much was at stake for so many. This might be the only time they could unwind before taking the train again to leave for Bratislava. The three men lifted their mugs to each other in a silent "*L'chaim* (To life)."

Later that night, Benny lay on his bed thinking of Varda. He tried to imagine her at work. He smiled into the darkness as he envisioned her getting on the motorcycle, going down the familiar dust road to a neighboring kibbutz. He wondered if she missed him as much as he longed to see her. It was during the quiet times at night, when alone, that he could really feel the ache and emptiness of missing her. He wished he could somehow let her know it was getting closer to the time when they could be together again. He took a deep breath, letting his muscles relax, and whispered into the silence: "A few more weeks and, with God's help, this mission will be over and we will all be home."

The days that followed went smoothly. Money for the train tickets arrived as scheduled, and the word was that things were going as planned with Storfer. The boats that were to take everyone down the Danube River to the Black Sea port of Tulcea, Romania, were going to arrive as promised.

Dora was beginning to feel the effects of her condition, along with being impatient. Both she and Jacob were anxious to reach Bratislava so they could be married. She and Betty, who had become close friends, enjoyed going to their favorite eatery where they would sit for as long as allowed.

It was on one of these outings that a frightening event happened. Dora and Betty were not aware that they were being observed as they ate near to a group of noisy German soldiers drinking beer. When the two girls left the eatery and stepped outside, two of the soldiers followed closely behind them, swaggering drunkenly. The anxious girls tried to walk faster, but the men caught up with them. One of the soldiers managed to grab hold of Dora. He shoved her roughly against a lamppost, while his friend laughed. Betty screamed for help. Dora kicked her drunken attacker, thrusting her knee between his legs. He doubled over in pain, groaning "Jew bitch!"

The other soldier stopped to console his partner. He shouted out to the terrified women, "Filthy Jew bitches!"

The girls ran into a shop to escape. They were too afraid to go back to the hotel immediately for fear of being followed.

Dora didn't want Jacob to know what had happened—there was no telling how he would react. But she found Benny and tearfully described the attack. He advised her and Betty not to tell anyone about the incident and comforted her, assuring her he would take care of it.

The following morning, warning notices were issued to everyone that no female would be allowed to go onto the streets of Prague without a male escort and there was to be a curfew. No reason was given except that Benny and Baruch had determined that it was no longer safe.

The days were uneventful and seemed long as everyone waited for notice to board the trains for Bratislava.

Finally, the evening came when Baruch was able to tell Benny and Shlomo that the next morning they were to begin preparing for departure from Prague.

"We'll be going in small groups each day," he explained. "The trains can't accommodate all three hundred of us at once. All tickets are to be handed out by individual group leaders. They will also advise each group when to pack and be ready to move out. Benny will leave with the first group."

Standing between the two men, Baruch placed his arms around their shoulders fondly. "We'll all be enjoying another train ride. This one takes us to Bratislava, and this, my friends, is the beginning of our journey home."

8

ARRIVING IN BRATISLAVA

There was a bus waiting at the train station when Benny arrived in Bratislava with the first group from Prague. The driver nodded without speaking.

After a short drive he pulled up in front of an old five-story brick building that sat a few hundred feet back from the main street. Turning to Benny, he spoke for the first time, in Slovak.

"This is it. There is no one here yet. You're the first to arrive, but there will be the Hlinka Guard stationed here later—you can count on it. They know you're coming. They know everything. Everything and everyone are under the control of the Germans."

Benny thanked him for his help offloading their bags.

The driver then gave a serious warning: "Be careful. They hate Jews."

Benny shook his hand. "I know. Thank you, my friend."

He stood for a minute looking at the building in front of him, then turned to those waiting in the parking area. "Well, come on. Let's go in and see what's inside."

Entering what was the lobby of the hostel, the young people set their bags on the floor. The shabby couch, with cushions that had long ago given in to the weight of people sitting on it, looked welcoming to Dora. Several padded chairs with fading flowers on a background of decaying fabric, held up by scarred legs, still looked sturdy to Benny, despite what he assumed were years of battles won against past guests. His invitation to "sit and relax while I look around" was eagerly accepted. This was going to be their lodging for the next few weeks.

Because of Bratislava's location on the Danube River, it was obvious to Benny that this had been a hostel set up to accommodate tourists as well as youth groups—how many in those parties he didn't know, but this group would be testing its capacity.

The large kitchen had food lockers, along with an oversized icebox. The room was stocked with pots and pans and everything needed to take care of cooking meals. There was a small bathroom just off the kitchen, making it handy for Rivka and those who would be working there. There was room for extra food storage if needed, along with other supplies, but most of the food would be purchased fresh from markets, and blocks of ice could be brought in from the local ice factory. Rivka would oversee the details for shopping as soon as possible. She and the others who would be purchasing food would have to get papers so they could shop in town. In the meantime, the leadership would be bringing in supplies later that day.

Benny stood in the middle of the dining room. *Meals will have to be served in shifts in this room*, he said to himself. *That won't be a problem, because everyone is used to working together and getting along.*

There were multiple beds lined up, dormitory style, in the basement of the building. The basement, along with the first two floors, would house the men, while the women would occupy the next three stories. Each floor had a bathroom at the end of its hallway, to be shared between the occupants of those rooms.

Over the next few days, others arrived without delays or incidents. Benny was glad to see Baruch and Shlomo. There was still much to be done.

Baruch, along with Benny and Shlomo, sat at a table in a corner of the kitchen. There were no preparations for the upcoming meal, so the kitchen was empty.

Baruch still made certain to speak low enough so that he couldn't be overheard.

"Jacob wants to make arrangements for him and Dora to get married as soon as possible. We're probably only going to be here for a few weeks so we will have to begin planning right away."

The other two men agreed.

Baruch continued. "Benny, you will have to contact a rabbi. I'll leave the wedding arrangements in your hands. Shlomo, try to figure out how we can bring some music in so we can make this a happy celebration for them. I'll talk with Rivka; I know she'll bake something for them. It's not going to be what Dora and Jacob would have under different circumstances, but we'll do our best."

Benny slapped Shlomo on the back: "Looks like you'll be warming up on the accordion, my friend." He became serious again. "I agree this is important. Dora's feeling very uncertain right now, and that worries Jacob. Once she sees that plans are underway, they'll both feel better."

"How do you think it will go with our Nazi security guards?" asked Baruch. "Can you keep them under some kind of control?"

Benny grinned. "As long as I can keep them in cigarettes and vodka, they'll behave, I'm sure. I actually think they might like me."

Baruch got to his feet. "Don't count on it, Benny. No Nazi will ever like a Jew, but if you can keep bribing them, we should be okay. Just be careful."

He shook hands with both men. "Thank you both. I'll meet with Jacob and Dora tonight." He paused for a moment. "This is a good thing! There's nothing like a wedding to lighten the mood for everyone."

Within a few days, plans were well underway. Jacob and Dora met with the rabbi, and there was going to be a wedding.

Benny stood in front of the *huppah*, the canopy where Jacob and Dora would stand before the rabbi that night. All of this and the past months had become his life—a life that left little time to think of Varda and their time together. Now, seeing the *huppah*, and sensing the happiness and the beginning of a life together that it symbolized, released emotions within him. Feelings of loneliness overwhelmed him for a moment as he thought of Varda. She, and the time they had spent together, seemed so far away. At that moment, all he wanted was to hold her close and love her. Taking a deep breath, he turned away. He wanted to check the room once more before the wedding. The space would definitely be crowded, with standing-room only; some guests would have to take the steps leading to the upper floors.

An area with a long table had been set apart from the *huppah* for the reception following the ceremony. Rivka covered the table with white cloth, then went outside and picked wild vines from alongside the hostel. She carefully placed the vines as decorative green barriers between large platters of freshly baked honey cakes and the bottles of wine brought in by Baruch. She also picked green leaves and scattered them over the white cloth where the glasses and dishes were placed. Benny was impressed with the beauty of what she had managed to accomplish with so little—and such little time.

There would not be a room set aside for the newlyweds because of the packed sleeping accommodations. Benny designated the couch for Jacob and Dora, moving it to a special seating area. Here they would sit together throughout the evening during the festivities.

Shlomo appeared, carrying an accordion and pretending to sing. "Let me serenade you, my friend!"

Benny laughed. "I can wait until tonight. Are you ready for this?"

Shlomo set the accordion down. "I forgot how heavy these things are," he muttered. "Samuel is bringing his violin. Between the two of us, we should be able to make music."

Benny slapped him on the back. "*Mazel tov*, my friend! If you can't, nobody can."

The Wedding Ceremony

The room was quiet as Baruch and Benny walked with Jacob through the crowded room toward the *huppah* to face the rabbi. Dora followed, accompanied by her sister and Betty.

Everyone in the room was somber as they listened to the rabbi's words. Each person had their own thoughts about a future that was still unknown.

After the reading of the wedding blessing and performing the marriage ceremony according to tradition, the rabbi blessed the couple and placed a wrapped wine glass on the floor in front of Jacob. When Jacob stepped on the glass, breaking it, there was a loud outcry—"*Mazel tov!*"—along with cheers from everyone. Both Jacob and Dora were crying, but the tears were tears of joy.

Handshakes and hugs of congratulations continued throughout the night. There was wine, honey cakes, music and laughter. At one point Shlomo and Samuel began playing "Hava Nagila." The room immediately filled with dancers.

Dora tugged on Jacob's arm. "Come on, my husband, let's dance! Let's celebrate our love and our life."

Jacob kissed her forehead. "This is your first request as my wife." He took her hand. "How can I refuse?"

They joined others in the dance. Baruch and Benny watched as the couple danced. Benny gave a salute, raising his glass to Baruch.

"This was a good thing," he said. Touching Baruch's glass, he made a toast: "To more good things!"

Baruch clicked his glass against Benny's. "*L'chaim!*"

Later that night after the others had gone to bed, Jacob and Dora sat together on the couch. They talked about the baby that was growing inside her, and shared plans for their life together as a family.

After a while, seeing that Dora was looking tired, Jacob took her hand in his. "Come, my wife, let's go to bed. It's been a wonderful evening."

He kissed her goodnight at the bottom of the steps, and Dora walked upstairs. He waited for several moments, then climbed the stairs to the room he was sharing with the other men.

9

THE LONG WAIT

Several weeks passed with no plans being made to leave the area. There was beginning to be some unrest within the hostel. Questions were asked that couldn't be answered.

Baruch decided to call a meeting, one he wasn't looking forward to. He had received notice that the money being sent by Jewish International to Berthold Storfer had been delayed for some unknown reason. He was also told that Storfer was still negotiating with Adolf Eichmann in Vienna regarding transportation. This was all the information he had and he knew it was not enough to satisfy those waiting for answers.

The reaction to this news was exactly what Baruch had expected. There was disbelief and confusion as Baruch shared what he knew. He had to be firm as he laid out the guidelines for the new situation.

"Because of the delay and because we don't know how much longer we will have to wait until the boats arrive, some of you will want to get out of the hotel from time to time, maybe to shop or just simply to get outdoors. Anyone wanting to leave the hotel will have to go to the head office of the Hlinka and get papers. You will have to do this each time you want to leave the hotel and move about. They already have a list of your names, so they will check your name off and give you a permit. You should always do this in a small group of no more than ten to avoid problems. Do *not* do this by yourself.

"Also, these permits are not to be confused with your travel papers. Your travel papers are issued only before leaving Bratislava and we will all have to get them soon enough. They are issued with an expiration date that needs to be updated regularly. We will wait until we have a better idea of what's going on before getting them. I know this is not what we planned. Like you, I was told we were going to be here for a short time—a few weeks, maximum. However, there is nothing we can do but wait and be calm. At least you will be able to leave this hotel, get out, and move about—something we didn't think was necessary before.

"I want you to remember why we have come this far and to remember where we are going. I trust in you not to be discouraged."

Later, Baruch met up with Benny. He told him about the delay, along with the young people's reaction to it.

Benny tried to encourage him. "Since I have no problem with travel permits, I can leave and go to Vienna. I will meet with Storfer. And I will contact Jewish International to see what the holdup is on the funds."

Baruch agreed. "I have to tell those who are paying for this hotel that we don't know how long it will be before we can leave."

Benny left early the next morning for Vienna. He returned a few days later after meeting with Storfer, bringing with him promises made by Storfer for the river-going boats: they were to arrive within weeks. These boats would take everyone down the Danube, to the port of Tulcea located on the Black Sea, and there the group would board ships that would take them to Palestine.

Immediately on his return, Benny had met with Baruch and told him about the deep suspicions within the organization about Storfer. Benny explained further.

"People are suspicious because of Storfer's close connections and success within the Austrian business community, along with his close connection to Eichmann. Because of their lack of trust and the huge amount of money being sent, they want to be certain that Storfer isn't playing each side."

Baruch frowned, showing his concern. "We have to get these young people out of here—they're going crazy."

Benny got to his feet.

"I know," he sighed. "I've got to get with our friends outside to see if they can't help to make life a little easier for these youngsters because they're feeling abandoned."

More weeks passed. Moods were serious, expressions more somber, as everyone waited to hear news of the boats. An occasional argument would erupt over simple things like chess or dominoes.

Dora spent most of her time in the bedroom, looking at the baby clothes—gifts sent to her by local Jewish women. Some days she would come down only for meals. Jacob could tell she was depressed. He tried to cheer her up with stories of a future they would share, but it was a future she could not see. She would listen, staring at him, her eyes pale and lifeless. She would offer no response. Jacob was concerned for her and the baby.

Weeks turned into months. The days became shorter. Rain, often turning to snow, made going out unpleasant. Eventually winter arrived, bringing bitter cold winds, along with more feelings of hopelessness and frustration. Conversations no longer included plans of leaving or the arrival of boats. Food was running low in the storage lockers. What food there was made Rivka's job harder. Meals were no longer the cheerful gatherings they once were.

Benny was in contact with local Jewish families who often supplied food to the hotel from their homes and local restaurants. They also brought in friends who were local musicians to play. But they had to be careful not to arouse the contempt of the guards positioned outside the hotel. On the occasions when they came to play, Benny provided the musicians with a bottle of cognac, telling them to give it to the guards when they arrived. Before long the guards were looking forward to their visits. In the meantime, Benny kept the on-duty guards supplied with cigarettes, along with the occasional bottle of vodka, hoping they would look the other way when members of the Jewish community arrived. He knew it was a risky game he was playing, but it was one he had to play.

The Promise of Spring and a New Life

Loud shrieks of pain could be heard from one of the bedrooms upstairs. Jacob ran up the steps and down the hall to where Dora was.

She lay crying on her bed. "The baby, the baby! I'm having the baby."

Jacob took her hand in his. "Try to be calm. I'll get someone."

She pushed his hand away. But when he turned to leave, she stopped him, yelling out in pain, "Don't leave me!"

Jacob looked at her face, stricken with fear. He couldn't leave her. He went to the door and called out as loud as he could, "Help! Get help! Dora is having the baby!"

Within minutes Betty and Sarah were in the room. Sarah put her hand on Jacob's chest. "Jacob, go down and get Rivka. Hurry."

He obeyed without comment. As he ran down the stairs, he stumbled, almost falling.

A few minutes later, Rivka appeared calm as she entered the bedroom. She quietly gave orders to Betty and Sarah: "Go to the kitchen and boil me a big pot of water. Get white cloths from the cupboard and bring them to me. Jacob, you go downstairs and wait—it will be okay. Dora will be all right." She smiled at him. "You are about to become a father."

Jacob kissed Dora's cheek. "I'll be close by, my love. Be brave. This is what we've been waiting for. I love you."

Once downstairs, Jacob began to weep uncontrollably, his entire body shaking. Seeing such a strong man broken and crying like this was shocking to the others in the room. It brought them abruptly out of their own solemn moods. One by one they approached Jacob, forming a circle of comfort around him.

Jacob was embarrassed. He had managed his entire life to keep his feelings to himself. Now he was suddenly crying and laughing at the same time, in a room full of people who were patting him on the back, comforting him and simultaneously congratulating him, while his wife was upstairs having his baby.

Betty and Sarah ignored the drama that was going on as they hurriedly carried cloths and pans of hot water from the kitchen, up the stairs to the bedroom. Rivka had managed to calm Dora, reassuring her with stories of how she had helped deliver babies at the kibbutz in Palestine.

Between pains, Dora was quiet as she listened. She asked Rivka to tell her more about the kibbutz. As Dora rested between contractions, Rivka gave more details about life on the kibbutz. She told Dora about Benny and his great love for Varda, and how hard it was for him to leave her.

Rivka's stories about Palestine and the kibbutz seemed to bring

Dora out from the dark place where she had been living for the past months. In between the pain of contractions, she asked Rivka questions, then smiled. "I'm going to love it there."

Rivka gently pushed the hair from Dora's damp forehead. "Yes—yes you will, and so will this little baby that's about to join us." She pushed gently on Dora's stomach, directing her, "Now, come on—work with me. Let's do this. Push!"

It was a soft command, which Dora followed. Sarah and Betty watched from across the room in awe. It was the first time they had witnessed anything like this.

Some time later, Rivka finished wrapping the baby in a clean white cloth, then told the girls to go downstairs to get Jacob. "Tell him to come up to see his wife and son."

The energy in the hotel following the birth of Jacob and Dora's baby was like the calm after a storm. Jacob's emotional response to Dora's giving birth, along with the arrival of the little boy, seemed to cause each person to remember, at least for the time being, what they had forgotten over the past months of isolation. They were still alive and they had one another. There was even lighthearted back-and-forth teasing like in the days at Osik.

The rabbi would be coming to do circumcision of the baby in eight days. Jacob told Baruch he would be honored if he would hold the baby during the *brith*.

"It will be a simple ceremony," he said. "Dora and I would like you to be his *sandek*."

Baruch was touched. This young man who had come to him as a lost boy, in search of a home, was now celebrating the birth of his child. To hold this baby, born in such a time as this, was like a gift.

He grabbed Jacob's shoulder fondly. "Thank you. The honor will be mine."

The two men shook hands.

Jacob grinned. "We've already given him a name, but we will introduce him to everyone after the *brith*."

Baruch chuckled. "Can't wait."

Jacob grabbed his hand again and shook it: "Great, just great!" He then left Baruch standing in the middle of the room where he had found him.

Looking around, Baruch said to himself, "With God's help, we have to get these people out of here."

Everyone gathered to witness the circumcision of the baby. There were smiles and lighthearted good wishes for Dora and Jacob. Rivka had managed to bake small rugelach cookies. She set up a table for coffee, even though there was no cream to serve with it. She filled pitchers with water for those who couldn't drink coffee without cream or milk, and there was wine for the celebration. No one seemed to mind about there being no cream. They complimented Rivka on the rugelach; it was something that hadn't been done before.

The ceremony was a simple one that included prayers by the rabbi and blessings by everyone in the crowded room. The baby cried.

Following the ceremony, Dora and Jacob turned with their backs to the rabbi and faced everyone. Jacob cradled the baby, carefully holding him so that he could be seen.

"Here he is, my friends," he announced. "Let me introduce you to our son. His name is Isaac."

A loud cheer filled the room. Benny turned to Shlomo: "You know what 'Isaac' means, don't you?"

Shlomo nodded, smiling. "Yes, it means laughter—'he shall laugh.'"

Weeks passed, then months, as those in the hotel waited. Dora would take Isaac downstairs to visit people each day, which helped the mood of those who played with him. He was growing fat from Dora's milk and was a happy baby. She would take him out to get sun in the backyard of the hotel, away from the guards, whenever possible. Summer had arrived and it was warm. She would let Isaac touch the grass and hold the flowers she picked. It was on these days she was happy.

The nights were warm now, sometimes making it difficult to sleep. One night Benny, after tossing and turning for what seemed like hours, got up and wandered into the kitchen, where he found Shlomo sitting on a chair, holding a glass of wine and a piece of bread. He teased, "Where did you find the wine, my friend?"

Shlomo raised his glass in a mock salute. "I can't sleep."

Benny pulled one of the chairs up beside him. "I know, it's hot—and you know, we got word that the boats we were promised will be on the way. There's a lot to think about now, all of a sudden."

Shlomo got to his feet. "Come on, let's go out back and sit. Maybe we'll catch a small breeze going by."

Benny poured himself a glass of wine. Shlomo picked up the bottle and the two men went outside. They sat on the cool steps, looking up at the dark sky, not saying anything for a few minutes. Benny was the first to speak.

"Shlomo, we've known each other our entire lives and I've never asked you: Why have you never talked about being interested in someone? Have you ever even thought you were in love?"

Shlomo waited, thoughtful for a minute, before answering.

"No, I've never met anyone that made me look twice." He

laughed quietly, then continued: "Well, I probably looked not once or twice but three or four times. I don't know . . . maybe I'm destined to be a bachelor for life. You're lucky to have met Varda."

Benny agreed. "Yes, but I had to go to Palestine to meet her. Maybe when we get back, you'll be struck by lightning like I was."

The wine was taking effect on the two men in the heat.

Shlomo laughed again. "How many wives did Solomon have? A thousand? Here I am, named after a king with how many wives?"

It was Benny's turn to laugh: "*Shlomo Hamelech*. Solomon the King. Wise King Solomon with his thousand wives and you, my friend, who were given his name, are without one serious love."

The two men talked until the sky was turning gray with the first signs of daybreak. They took their glasses to the kitchen and said they would meet later for breakfast. It had been a long night, but a good night, for both men. They had reminisced about being old friends, without any talk of German oppression and boats not showing up or plans not going as planned. There would be time enough for that.

Finally, Good News

Baruch was waiting for Benny when he came down for breakfast. He handed him the telegram he had received from Storfer: "The river-going boats will be arriving from Vienna in two weeks without delay."

Benny looked at the telegram and handed it back.

Looking at each other, the two men gave in to showing their excitement: "Can you believe it?"

Each answered at the same time, "Yes, we can believe it! The boats are coming and we're getting these people out of here. Thank God!"

Benny called for a meeting with his group leaders.

"Organize your people in small groups of fifteen," he instructed. "They will be going to the Hlinka headquarters to get their travel certificates for departure. There has been a telegram from Adolf Eichmann's office sent to the Hlinka HQ, so assure our people it will be okay. However, they will have to wait while the certificates are being processed. Tell them to be patient."

Shlomo was holding duplicate meetings with his own group leaders.

Meanwhile there was excitement running through the entire hotel. There was laughter and animated talking among the young people. Women were hugging men and one another. Men were hugging other men, some crying openly, unashamed.

Jacob grabbed Dora, who was holding little Isaac. He swung them around, shouting "I told you, I told you—we're going to Palestine! We're going home!"

A startled Isaac started crying. The shouting and swinging around frightened him.

Dora pulled herself away from Jacob's arms, scolding him. "Stop it! You're scaring him to death." She left the room, trying to calm the baby.

Jacob watched her leave, then grabbed someone else who was standing close by and swung him around, shouting, "We're going home!"

Laughing, the two men continued to dance in a circle. Almost at once, others joined them until the circle of joyful dancers filled the room. Many ended up exhausted, some falling into chairs, others falling onto the floor laughing.

Baruch had been watching the entire thing from where he was standing. Thinking aloud, he murmured: "Let them dance. God knows they deserve this good news."

Benny returned later from meeting with his group leaders; Shlomo hadn't returned yet. Benny found Baruch in the kitchen.

"Now we hold our breath," he said, "and hope everything goes as planned."

Baruch agreed. "It's going to take these next few weeks to get everyone their travel certificates."

Day after day, coordinated small groups left the hotel to stand in line at the Hlinka headquarters, where a list of names was checked off. Each travel document was stamped with a German swastika. Hlinka officers smirked as they handed them to those who were waiting. The insults were accepted quietly, along with the certificates that would give them permission to leave Bratislava. Once back at the hotel, the lucky ones waited anxiously for the others to return.

Everyone finally received their travel documents. Now they would prepare to leave, as they waited for the boats to arrive. It would be necessary to take enough food and supplies to accommodate everyone. The trip on the Danube River was calculated to take one week. Each group leader would oversee the gathering of supplies, along with how to transport them to the boats. The mood was quiet, with little interaction, as they waited now to hear that the boats had arrived.

Dora often remained in the room upstairs, spending her time with Isaac, who at six months old was happily unaware of what was going on around him. She had promised herself that she would expose this child, whom she loved more than her own life, to as much love and laughter as was possible.

Jacob had also made a promise. When his son was born, an emotional Jacob had sworn to Dora: "He will never feel lost, afraid, or forgotten."

Both promises would be tested to their limits.

9

LEAVING BRATISLAVA

Benny met with Baruch and Shlomo in the kitchen. The boats had arrived and were docked. It was time to leave. Before leaving they would have to meet with the other group leaders to organize and ensure a smooth departure. They still had to avoid as much attention as possible.

Jacob helped Dora gather clothes for themselves, along with rags from torn sheets that would become diapers for the baby. They would take only the minimum for themselves. Food for everyone during the trip down the Danube had been arranged by Rivka.

Everything was ready now for their departure. There was almost an eerie quiet as groups systematically placed their belongings on the floor and stood beside them in silence, waiting to leave this place that had kept them captive for months.

Darkness was setting in. A heavy mist hung over the banks of the Danube River. The reflections of magnificent trees along the banks of the Danube had lost their beauty in the fading light and fog. They appeared now as ominous shadows on the water.

The three men watched as hundreds of ghost-like figures made their way silently up the gangplanks onto the boats. Also watching the eerie processions taking place were Hlinka guards, their guns aimed and ready should anyone decide to escape. Every so often you could hear, through the fog, a low muffled command from one of the group leaders from the other three boats along the shoreline.

Hundreds of refugees, young and old alike, from other areas had been gathered together and were boarding the four river-going boats. Finally, the gangplanks were about to be taken down.

Benny spoke for the first time since they had arrived at the shore.

"Okay, my friends, we're on this boat together."

With that, he jumped aboard the first vessel, along with Baruch and Shlomo.

Hundreds of bodies were crowded together on the deck. This old tourist boat had carried many a load of happy tourists up and down the Danube River for years. Now it was transporting these desperate souls from a place of hopelessness to a country where the promise of a new life would begin.

Benny moved through the packed bodies toward the stern of the boat. He discovered there were two cabins that could be used for some of the women who had babies. He made his way slowly, searching for Jacob and Dora. After much angling and worming through the crowds, he finally spotted Jacob.

Dora was crowded against a rail, holding her baby tightly against her chest as she tried to keep her balance. Benny took her arm.

"Come with me," he said firmly. "I'm taking you and little Isaac to a cabin."

Dora allowed him to lead her without question.

Once in the cabin, Benny explained: "It will be crowded here too. Other women with babies will join you, but it will be better for you and Isaac in here. Jacob will be with me. Once we get to the ships' harbor, we will make sure you are with him again."

Benny hoped he had been able to calm her fears. He knew Dora was a strong woman, but he also realized that the past months, along with everything she had witnessed and endured, had left her shaken. She continued to cling tightly to her baby.

Benny slapped Jacob on the back. "It doesn't look like there's going to be much room to lie down." He laughed. "Have you ever slept standing up?" Then he became serious again. "We need your help, Jacob. This isn't going to be an easy trip for anyone. We have to help these people to remember that this is our passageway to freedom."

Benny made his way to the top deck where the captain was. He wasn't sure what kind of reception he would get. He knew that the crew were German and the boat was sailing under the German flag. The captains, whether German or Slovak, had been paid with Jewish funds by Storfer in Vienna. They were to ferry the boats from Bratislava to the Black Sea port. After seeing the age and condition of the boat they were on, Benny wasn't going to be surprised at anything.

Tapping on the door of the cabin, he waited. The command to enter was in Slovak.

Benny introduced himself. He explained that he was assigned to help should any problems arise on the trip. The captain was noncommittal. Benny asked about the calculated time of arrival at the port, again without any committed response. The captain smirked as he told Benny they would definitely be encountering German patrol boats on the river.

This information, offered with such obvious pleasure by the captain, was no surprise to Benny. Now there was no doubt in his mind about the captain. Sadly, the man had control of this vessel with hundreds of lives on board.

Benny thanked him and left to join Jacob, who had been waiting outside the cabin. He kept his thoughts to himself.

Baruch made his way to the area that was going to be allocated for food distribution. Quantities of food would have to be strictly controlled so they wouldn't run out. Even if everything went well, meals would be meager.

He met up with Rivka as she was taking stock of what was available, which wasn't much. The bread and sausages, along with powdered eggs, canned meat and fish, would have to last for the entire trip. She had managed to include some apples, but they would be eaten only if the other food was running out. Some of the older refugees arriving from Vienna and Danzig had smuggled items aboard in their pockets and bags. Sharing would be up to them. These refugees also sometimes needed special foods to sustain themselves, whereas the young could get by on less.

Special sleeping arrangements had to be considered for some elderly passengers. It was obvious that many of the older refugees who had boarded were in trouble physically and emotionally. The young were going to have to hold up the weak and frail.

Shlomo walked to the side of the boat with Jacob, as far away from the others as possible. He spoke in a low voice, just loud enough to be heard by the younger man.

"This is much bigger than we expected, Jacob. This goes way beyond us. Some of these people are lost and confused; others are already sick and probably should be hospitalized. How they made it here I don't know. We have to somehow guide them to areas where they will be safe. There's not even space for them to sit, let alone lie down. Let's sort them out and get them away from all the pushing and shoving, and the noise. We can move the younger immigrants to the upper deck."

Jacob agreed, then told Shlomo he wanted to check on Dora and little Isaac.

He left Shlomo and made his way through a maze of bodies to the cabin, where he found Dora curled up around a sleeping baby on one of the beds. The cabin was filled to capacity now. Jacob did his best to ignore the old woman who was rocking back and forth on one of the beds. She was weeping as she prayed aloud in Yiddish. He recognized the prayer as a plea for death. Looking around the cabin at the faces of these women, he remembered for a moment the face of his mother.

He forced himself to smile at the passengers.

"Well, good news!" he said brightly. "It won't be much longer now, will it?"

He hoped this would give them hope.

Benny leaned against the rail, taking in a deep breath as he looked around the crowded space in front of him. He took another deep breath, telling himself "*Mazel tov*," and began to move through a wall of refugees. There was praying going on, mixed with weeping, along with some arguments. Some of the older refugees were Orthodox Jews and had contempt for those they viewed as having no belief. At the same time, those non-practicing Jews viewed the Orthodox as religious fanatics. Even under these circumstances, they couldn't bond.

The younger groups were more positive, and talking among themselves. Benny was aware that these young people were looking at this situation as an adventure. The sacrifices made by their parents, and their time in Osik, had protected them from experiencing what others here had been subjected to on the streets and in their homes.

Baruch agreed with Benny when he suggested they could use the positive energy of the young people to somehow revitalize the older refugees. They gathered the younger immigrants into small groups. Baruch, along with Benny and Shlomo, met separately with these small groups to share their plan.

"Each individual group will spread out among the older refugees," Benny explained to the young people gathered around him. "You will help them with blankets to stay warm. And make sure everyone is given food."

He also said plainly: "It is almost certain that some of these older immigrants will not survive until we reach our homeland. We have to do everything we can to keep them with us."

The usually calm Benny became emotional at hearing his own words. He climbed onto a table, where he stood for a moment to regain his composure.

Baruch noticed this and looked at Shlomo. "What's he doing?" he asked.

Shlomo shrugged. "I guess we'll find out."

Benny's Emotional Speech

Benny stared into the faces in front of him. He saw the Orthodox, the non-religious, the wealthy, and the poor. He saw the old and the young, the weak and the strong. These were the dreamers and the disillusioned. Somehow, he had to reach them.

His throat was dry and his voice was hoarse with emotion as he spoke.

"Here we are!" he began. "Welcome."

He waited. There was no response.

He continued. "We are all here on a mission to reach our homeland, Eretz Israel."

A voice from somewhere in the crowd shouted, "We don't even know if it's real! Maybe we're going through this hell for nothing!"

The voice had come from somewhere behind those directly in front. Looking over the heads of those surrounding him, searching for the faceless voice, Benny's response was immediate.

"Oh it's real. Believe me, I've been there." He hesitated a minute, then continued with a question. "Do you know what else is real? The Nazis whose flag we are sailing under right now—those same Germans who want us all to disappear. But let me tell you, we are not going to disappear! They don't know who our forefathers were and they don't know who *we* are!"

He was angry now. Baruch and Shlomo were in shock. Dora had joined Jacob on the deck above, with little Isaac, and the two stood transfixed as they listened.

Benny continued: "They want to beat us into our graves, but we will win! And do you know how we will win? I know how we will win. We will win by *living*. We will stay alive and we will survive. This is how we win."

There was a sharp cry from somewhere: "We will live! We will live!"

The words "We will live" suddenly became a chant, over and over . . . Then something amazing happened. The young refugees began to sing. It was almost as if it were pre-planned. Their voices came together in unison from separate locations on the boat as they sang "Hatikva," the song they all knew and loved. The words were coming from everywhere on the boat. Many tried singing along in their own language; others listened with tears streaming

115

down their faces. Voices carrying the words could be heard by every refugee.

Benny sat down, his head in his hands, weeping. He was crying unashamedly. He cried for those souls on board. He cried for those who wouldn't make it and he cried out of his loneliness for Varda.

No one mentioned Benny's emotional outburst after his outcry to the refugees. Benny said nothing to Baruch or Shlomo. Between the three men, it was as if it had never happened. His words did have an effect, however.

The next days were without incident. The younger refugees on board looked after those who needed care. There were friendly conversations happening. Young and old alike enjoyed the scenery as the boat glided over the still waters of the Danube. The calm among the refugees continued, even when German patrols ran alongside the boats through those Yugoslavian territories that were not yet under German control. Those on board were actually thankful to be sailing under the swastika flag.

Dora often took Isaac to the deck where she would show him the tree-lined shores and make certain he was exposed to the fresh air and sunshine. His animated baby-talk and laughter entertained those around him, and Dora enjoyed sharing him with others.

More days passed. All anyone could do was try to remain as comfortable as possible. They did this by exchanging space. Those sitting gave up their position to others who had been standing for long hours. Those who were close to the outer rails relinquished their views to others in an effort to break the monotony.

Baruch checked on food supplies with Rivka. The food was running out. It was Shlomo's job to explain the situation, and it wasn't going to be easy. It was now necessary that small amounts of whatever was available would be distributed among the older and weaker passengers. The young and healthy would take only enough every few days to sustain themselves. Water was limited.

More days passed. The only food left amounted to a few pieces of dried bread that were broken into portions not much bigger than crumbs. Almost everyone on board was weak; others were sick. Benny once again took to his stance on the bench in an effort to encourage people. His voice sounded strong and filled with confidence as he spoke.

"We are about to cross the finish line, my friends! We are almost there. Breathe deeply now. Fill your lungs with the fresh air of freedom. I want you to save your energy for when we board the ship. Think about it! You had the strength of the lion. You did it! You made it!"

There were cheers as he stepped down. Baruch and Jacob shook hands with Benny. Shlomo hugged him, laughing: "You're right— we did it, didn't we?"

Dora chuckled as little Isaac reached his tiny hands toward Benny.

"Look!" she said. "Even the baby wants to thank you."

Benny took the baby into his arms and kissed him on the cheek before giving him back to his mother.

"We should be arriving in port tomorrow," he told them all. "Let's get ready to leave this floating trap. I want to go up and thank our captain for a safe journey."

Benny made his way to the upper deck. It had been a long voyage since the first time he had knocked on this door.

The captain issued a command to enter.

Benny strode into the cabin and smiled warmly.

"Captain, I want to thank you and your crew for a safe journey and tell you *Tschuss* (Bye)."

The look on the captain's stern face didn't change as he answered, "*Tschuss.*"

Benny extended his arm to shake hands. The captain's face remained expressionless. He rejected Benny's hand.

Benny nodded goodbye and left the cabin, ignoring the obvious act of hostile rejection. Once outside, he shook his head and smiled to himself, saying softly, "*Shalom.*"

Where Are the Ships?

Dawn was breaking the next morning when the refugees glimpsed the hillsides of the Romanian city of Tulcea. But as the boat glided into port, they were disappointed to see that the ships they were to board were not anchored in the harbor as they expected. Because it was early morning, however, the passengers reassured themselves that the promised ships would be arriving later in the day or possibly even during the night. They were happy to have arrived safely at Tulcea.

There was very little activity in the port, with the exception of workers involved with what looked to be heavy carpentry on the decks of some old ships anchored by the dock. The refugees watched with curiosity while men carried heavy planks aboard one of these rusty vessels. They idly wondered what was being built on the deck of a disused ship that had no flag and no name painted on its rusted bow. With nothing else to do, they viewed the activity as work continued on the decks of the three old abandoned ships.

Morning turned into afternoon. People grew tired of watching as nightfall approached and quiet overtook the port. Those on board fell into a troubled sleep. The promised ships that were going to take them to Palestine had still not arrived.

The following morning as the sun rose, Benny stood on the upper deck looking into the harbor. The sun glistened on the water;

the air was crisp and clear. He took a deep breath, taking in the activity of the port. What he saw next both shocked and angered him. The three rusted ships, thought to have been abandoned, had been painted, complete with names on their hulls. The carpentry work, finished the day before, was unmistakably visible on the decks. Each ship was now flying a Panamanian flag from its mast.

It was hard for Benny to keep his composure as he searched for Baruch and Shlomo.

He found Shlomo first. Grabbing his friend by the shoulders, he turned him around to face the ships. His voice was a fierce whisper: "Do you see what Storfer did?"

Shlomo looked at the ships. He couldn't believe what he was seeing.

"What are we going to do?" he cried, immediately answering his own question: "Nothing. There's nothing we can do."

Baruch joined the two men beside the railing.

"We have to unload the refugees now," he told them urgently. "The captains want to get everyone off the boats so they can go back to transporting Germans for the Reich."

Benny thought for a minute before reacting. "They will start offloading all the boats as quickly as possible. It's going to cause mass confusion and panic unless we work quickly to take control. We have no choice and we're going to need all the help we can get."

11

SHIP OF TERROR

The old ship looked dark and ominous as it waited for the first set of passengers to board. The vessel had no crew. Its engines were quiet.

The captains aboard the boats were shouting orders for everyone to begin offloading. Benny saw that a second boat had pulled alongside the ship, which meant that refugees from that boat would be disembarking, along with those from the one they were on, making the situation even worse.

He yelled across to one of the leaders on the second boat, "How many are you offloading?"

The voice yelled back, "They told us half."

"How many is half?" Benny responded, even though he was certain there had to be at least the same number of refugees on that boat. But there wasn't time for an answer before the captain on the second boat ordered its passengers to begin offloading. Benny could see the chaotic action begin as people started separating themselves from others in an effort to be first. He had feared there was not going to be time for an orderly exchange and he was right.

There was no organized control, as old and young alike moved like a river of human bodies from the boats onto the ship. They moved slowly, pushing their way to wherever the force of movement took them, into areas unknown. Again like a river, some moved down to the lower levels, where stacked wooden shelves had been built to serve as sleeping quarters. The shelves had been covered in straw that made breathing difficult because of the lack of air circulation. The lower area of the ship was like a dark cavernous hole that reeked with the smell of mold.

After seeing the circumstances below, many tried to go against the tide of bodies to reach the upper deck where there was air to breathe. This caused even more chaos. Some of the old and weak fell beneath the crushing flood of bodies. Others stumbled over those who had fallen, as they were forced forward by the movement behind them.

At long last, the motion stopped. Boarding was complete.

Benny had remained on board the boat, along with Baruch and Shlomo, to make certain that everyone was safely transferred onto the *Atlantic*. The three men now boarded the ship, and were horrified at what they saw.

Benny leaned toward Shlomo and Baruch. "My God!" he exclaimed. "These poor people are packed in like human sardines! What were they thinking in Vienna?"

Baruch's answer was one that they, along with everyone else on the ship, would become familiar with: "They didn't care."

Those aboard the *Atlantic* would have to live with it or die with it.

Benny worked his way toward the engine room to check it out. Baruch had left, setting out to find Rivka and some of the young refugees. Shlomo in the meantime had told Benny he was going to look for Jacob and Dora.

Benny stood in the engine room for several minutes, looking at the furnace and rusted fittings. From there he made his way down the ladder to see what had been converted into berthing areas. There were no lights, but he managed to see the cramped spaces between bunks. He crawled onto one of the bunks and tried to sit up, hitting his head. Lying down again, he could measure the space for movement where someone would lie—there was none. The dust and smell of mold from the straw was intense.

Leaving there, he walked the crowded passageways. There were children with their parents crowded into every corner of the ship, people lying along the passageway walls, while others were leaning wherever they could find a space. Benny reached down, patting the head of a child as he passed. The child did not respond.

He kept walking. He had to focus on trying to find a solution to this nightmare.

Someone had urinated on the floor. An old man looked at him sheepishly as he passed. Benny touched his shoulder in a kind gesture, shaking his head: "It's okay. Don't worry about it." But he asked himself angrily, *How can people find the bathrooms? And if they do find them, how can they use them if they need them? Are they animals? Where is the dignity in all this?*

Benny found himself walking faster until he was almost running. He had to find Baruch. They had to get this madness under control.

When he found him, he shared all he had seen, including the state of the engine room.

"There is no coal for the furnace," he reported. "There are not enough lifebelts or lifeboats. These people will be trying to find their way in darkness because there are no lights. There are not enough toilets, and even those few toilets don't work because there's no water to flush them." He was almost shouting now. "Do you know that I saw a poor man in tears, peeing on the floor, humiliated? We have to make this right somehow!"

Baruch listened, allowing Benny to vent his anger. He told him that he and Shlomo thought of having the young refugees work at monitoring the situation. This was the only way to go. They needed people to separate the groups requiring special help from the stronger ones, as well as those with children. Benny agreed. They would also make sure the few cabins available would be used for women and children.

Shlomo told them that when he talked just now with Jacob and Dora, Jacob had said he would not leave his wife and son to fight this chaos alone. He would remain with them until things settled down and he knew they were safe. Because he could not enter the women's cabin himself, he would stand or sit nearby, making sure they were taken care of.

Benny understood Jacob's need to protect his wife and son. He also understood that there were other fathers and mothers on board, helpless with small children, who were feeling the same way. He would have Jacob organize a safe place for children to be with one parent; that parent would ensure the safety and care of the child. After Benny told Baruch and Shlomo what he was thinking, and they agreed, he left to find Jacob.

There was nothing they could do immediately. The chaos would have to continue for now. The three men, along with Rivka, worked throughout the night. By morning, although exhausted, they had a plan.

The plan to use the help of the younger refugees worked. Life was now a controlled chaos instead of the previous panic. But, regardless of how much people cooperated with one another, conditions were not going to get better until the ship sailed. Below, the air was hot and heavy with damp mold, making it impossible to breathe. Benny hoped this would change once the engines were running. In the meantime it would be necessary to make room above and arrange for people to take shifts sleeping, as they had done on the boats.

There was a low grumbling among some when they heard of this arrangement, while others accepted the situation quietly. They realized that sleeping exposed to the elements, even crowded together and not being able to move, was better than suffocating below in total darkness. At least they could get a glimpse of sky and breathe fresh air. This was not the case for everyone, however.

Inside, cramped bodies were everywhere. They were in passageways, on stairs, under tables and on top of tables in what was supposed to be a dining room. The only spaces without bodies were the five bathrooms on board. That was because of the stench and standing water with feces from toilets that had overflowed.

The captain and crew had not boarded yet. Several days went by without news from Storfer. The *Atlantic* was still without a captain or a crew. Benny could not leave the ship. They were all at the mercy of Storfer and his willingness or his ability to get things moving.

Rivka, and the others in charge of seeing that people were fed, worked tirelessly, passing out small quantities of the meager supplies they had. This amounted to old bread, fruit, and tea that had been made with rancid water from the ship's barrels. Although disgusting, everything was accepted gratefully. Those who in the beginning saw themselves as not willing to sacrifice their personal eating habits were soon humbled. They accepted their status without complaint; hunger was a common bond now.

Benny and Baruch, along with Shlomo, decided to check out a space where a door had been left unlocked. They believed it could be an empty storage room and they were right. Other than a pile of small boards, there was little else except some empty paint-buckets, along with old paintbrushes piled in one corner. The three looked at the buckets, then at one another.

A surprised Shlomo stared at the pile. "There must be at least a couple dozen buckets here."

Baruch gave a closer look. "The paint dried up long ago," he said, "maybe even years ago. These buckets can be used as portable bathrooms."

Shlomo threw his arms up. "It's a miracle!"

The men laughed. They were pleased with the discovery and amused at Shlomo's reaction.

Benny suggested they get a few of the younger males to clean out the buckets right away so they could be put to good use.

"Discovering these buckets was a good thing," he said, "but I have a feeling we're going to need to discover more."

A Ship without a Captain

There was still no captain or crew, and no reasonable explanation as far as Benny was concerned. For now, he would concentrate on making certain that provisions for food and water, along with medicines, would be brought aboard as promised. These were items that had been paid for in advance.

A representative for Storfer arrived one morning, introducing himself only as Herm Goldner. During further conversation, he told Benny that he was actually related to Storfer by marriage and was representing him in all of his business affairs in Tulcea. Benny found him to be a bit confused and not up to date as far as details previously arranged. Goldner also spoke about the possibility of a war and how the British were considering halting all immigrations of Jews to Palestine.

Benny listened politely, then asked the only questions that as far as he was concerned needed to be answered: "When are we getting what was promised, paid for, and committed to? When are my people going to leave this harbor? Where is the captain and where is the crew? Where is the food we paid for?"

Benny's voice was calm, without emotion, as he continued. "I don't give a damn about anything except getting my people out of this harbor, onto the sea, and to their destination. You tell whoever you have to tell: I will make sure that those I represent in Palestine make certain your brother-in-law keeps his word, and so far, from what I've witnessed, he hasn't done a good job of that. I will expect something to change—and change quickly."

Herm Goldner nodded uncomfortably.

Benny smiled at him and extended his arm to shake hands. "Good luck."

Day-to-day life aboard the *Atlantic* had settled into a calm acceptance of misery and waiting. It was announced that a fourth ship would be arriving, complete with provisions and crew. It would be joining the other ships and would take on some passengers from the *Atlantic* to relieve the pressure. Benny assumed that his conversation with Mr. Goldner had been effective.

A few days later Storfer himself came aboard to meet with Benny. He explained that the British had earlier threatened to seize any ship in the territorial waters of Palestine that was carrying illegal immigrants, and imprison the captain and crew. The British

Consulate had pressured those who were hired in Piraeus to break their contracts. He went on to tell Benny how difficult it was to get a captain and crew because people were afraid.

Benny listened, then thanked Storfer for coming aboard, but continued the conversation.

"You have to know what has happened here," he said firmly. "We are imprisoned on a ship that we don't even know will be seaworthy by the looks of everything. The conditions are deplorable and there is no food or water or sanitary facilities. People are sick and they will die. Look around you! Better yet, come with me. Let me show you."

He led an unwilling Storfer through the passageways, down the stairs, and into the cavernous lower belly of the ship. At one point Storfer attempted to stop, but Benny encouraged him. "Keep going. We haven't seen the bathrooms. And we're going to stop for tea and bread with Rivka. Our food is your food."

It was obvious to Benny that Storfer was getting nauseous—and he hadn't seen the toilets yet. Benny was enjoying making the man suffer during his visit. He wanted to make certain that Storfer understood what everyone aboard this ship was experiencing, every hour of every day.

Rivka offered tea and a small piece of bread but wasn't surprised that it was turned down.

As they walked back through the crowded bodies of angry people lined against the paneled walls of the ship, Storfer tried to ignore the remarks made toward him. He was visibly shaken and sick.

Benny knew he wanted to escape. He extended his hand.

"Thank you, Mr. Storfer, for taking the initiative to meet with me in person instead of leaving this to your relative. You can see now, firsthand, what needs to be done. You're a smart man and I know that. I'm sure you are capable of doing whatever is needed to get this ship out of the harbor and on its way." He patted Storfer's shoulder. "*Mazel tov.*"

Storfer shook Benny's hand and left.

After he was gone, Benny had a strong urge to see little Isaac, and decided to look for Jacob and Dora. He found them sitting on the floor outside one of the cabins with a group of mothers and their children. He took the baby into his arms, hugging him tightly. He needed to feel this innocent baby in his arms and remember what it was like to love.

Those aboard were becoming accustomed to their discomfort and daily hunger. Benny was impressed with their remarkable resilience.

One day, one of the men approached Benny, telling him that he had been a practicing doctor before the Nazis forced him out of his office onto the streets. Benny knew there must be more stories like his among those on board. Anyone having medical experience of any kind was therefore encouraged to come forward. An infirmary was set up, even though there were no supplies. Benny believed that having a doctor available and nursing care, even without supplies, would offer hope to those who were feeling helpless, and hope was what was needed. He couldn't help but think of the clinic back home and Varda.

More time passed since Storfer's visit. Friendships that had been formed in Bratislava became even stronger, and new friendships were being formed with others who had boarded from the second boat. Life was taking on a kind of acceptance, making it easier to look forward.

There were still illnesses brought on by conditions aboard the ship. All of these health issues had to be taken seriously. The staff in the infirmary did what they could. Cleanliness was not something even to be considered, since there was no water for washing. Constantly being exposed to the floor of the ship, along with the elements, created undeniable skin problems and open sores. Some of the children developed dysentery, while many older people were battling with anxiety and depression. There were also some elderly refugees with bronchitis that threatened to become pneumonia.

Dawn was just breaking as Benny walked the passageways of the ship. It was not an uncommon habit for him to check on the status of everyone who was sleeping. Suddenly he almost stumbled over the frail body of someone lying on the floor. Bending down to apologize, he became aware the man was not sleeping. He had obviously died sometime during the night.

The man's thin body made it possible for Benny to lift him. He placed the man over his shoulder and carried him away as quickly and quietly as possible so as not to disturb those around him who hopefully might still be asleep.

There was a bench outside of the infirmary where Benny gently laid the man on his back. Baruch had to be told. They had to figure out what to do with this poor soul. The dead could not be buried at sea when the ship was not yet out of the harbor. This was a problem they had not previously had to deal with. There were no sheets aboard to wrap him in. But they would have to wrap or cover him with something.

The smell of damp mold and straw made it difficult to breathe, so there was no talking as the three men entered the hold, where they knew the makeshift bunks were. With outstretched arms in front of them, they made their way in silence through the darkness until they bumped into what seemed to be a row of beds with straw mattresses. Groping around with their hands in the darkness, they felt what they thought was a mattress, and pulled at it. Once they had control of the bulky bundle, they turned around awkwardly, taking small shuffling steps back in the direction they believed they had come.

At the bottom of the ladder, they could see for the first time and breathe.

Shlomo dropped his bundle on the floor in front of him and bent over, coughing. "No one can survive down there."

Baruch and Benny agreed. The two men tore open the canvas that was holding the straw. It was easy to do because it had only been stapled at one end. After pulling out all the straw, they left it on the floor to be picked up later. They then carried the canvas up to where the body of the man lay. It was still early, and Benny hoped that no one had made their way to the infirmary yet.

Thankfully, the area was empty. Making sure all of the staples were out of the canvas, Baruch and Benny shook it to remove any remaining straw and placed it so the body was completely covered. They then said a prayer in solemn silence for this man, whose name they did not know.

The fourth ship was spotted as it anchored in the harbor a few days later. It was a much smaller vessel than the *Atlantic* and looked to be in need of major repairs. Even so, its appearance caused excitement because this was the ship that was rumored to have provisions and food aboard, along with a captain and crew.

Benny had been told that 500 of those on board the *Atlantic* would be transferred to this other ship. That would mean it would have to be repaired and altered to accommodate those passengers, meaning more delay.

Storfer made himself available to Benny while coal and other provisions, including lifebelts, were being loaded onto the ship. He notified Benny that the small vessel could not take on any of the *Atlantic*'s passengers because it needed repairs.

He continued with his monologue: "Unfortunately, there are some shortages due to rumors of war. Food is being reserved for the armies. You will have to conserve even more than planned."

Benny had an urge to grab Storfer by the jacket and toss him overboard. But he maintained a look of calm as he listened to the excuses being laid out.

Storfer went on: "The *Atlantic* will have to make a stop on the way to pick up more coal and any provisions needed. You'll probably have to anchor out of Istanbul and do some negotiating."

Benny let him finish talking before speaking. "We will be raising anchor though, right?"

Storfer nodded. "Yes, the captain has assured me." The captain and crew had finally boarded the ship.

Storfer said his final words: "Have a safe journey."

Benny watched as the businessman spoke to the captain for a few minutes, then left the ship.

Benny turned his attention to the motley-looking crew. The men were bringing aboard separate quantities of food and what looked like liquor, which was taken to their quarters. It was obvious to him that the ship was going to be in unscrupulous hands.

The captain and most of the crew were Greek. Benny, speaking in Greek, introduced himself to the captain, who returned his own introduction in the same language, giving his name as Spiro.

The captain continued to speak in Greek: "How many immigrants do you have aboard this ship?"

Benny wondered why he was asking the question. He answered,

"We have eighteen hundred souls aboard this ship."

The next morning there was some activity among the crew. The furnaces were stoked with coal, and it wouldn't be long now before the boilers would be hot. However, the engines would not be started until the last moment to conserve fuel, so there was still no electricity aboard.

Everyone waited for signs that would tell them they were leaving port. There was an excited murmuring of voices in the quiet darkness.

"Listen, do you hear that?"

"They're getting ready . . ."

Then once again quiet, as they continued to wait.

Baruch had to inform Rivka and the others working with her that there was going to be less food than they had counted on. They might be without supplies the last week, before arriving in Israel. They would need to ration even more than she had planned.

This news didn't seem to faze Rivka. Patting Baruch on his shoulder, she laughed. "Do you think we can't handle this? Not to worry, my friend. All we have to do is get there—we won't worry about being a little hungry."

Baruch grinned. "I knew you could handle it. I wasn't worried."

Now he had to find Shlomo, who was at the infirmary. Shlomo had developed a cough and had been having trouble breathing since dealing with the straw mattresses. The doctor thought it was possible that he had taken something into his lungs and was having him inhale warm steam several times a day. Benny was concerned. He had to argue with Shlomo to make him take the doctor's advice.

Later that afternoon, everything stopped. The crew disappeared into their cabins.

The captain came looking for Benny, yelling and waving his arms.

"I won't do this!" he exclaimed. "You've got too many people. You've got to get rid of some of these refugees."

Benny was calm. "I agree, Spiro. You are absolutely right, but why are you telling me this now? Nothing has changed since Storfer was aboard and he refuses to put people on another ship. What can we do?"

Spiro looked down, avoiding Benny's gaze.

"I don't know," he muttered. "Maybe I can talk to the crew, see if maybe they'll agree. It will be a lot of work. Maybe we'll have to take everything off except your people."

Benny thought for a minute before replying.

"I can't let you take my people's belongings, Spiro. It's all they have that's left of their life. I can offer your crew some compensation, though, for their hard work."

He waited, pretending to let Spiro consider his offer, one he knew the captain would accept on behalf of his crew. He also knew there was a good possibility the crew would never see any compensation.

The offer was accepted graciously.

The next morning, a much more friendly Captain Spiro advised Benny that the port authority of Tulcea had issued a certificate for the *Atlantic* to leave the harbor.

Benny shook the captain's hand forcefully. "Great news, Captain. Good job."

The captain smiled. "Tell your people we'll raise anchor tomorrow morning."

The Voyage Begins

True to the captain's word, the *Atlantic* raised anchor—to the sound of cheers from everyone on board. Benny, along with Shlomo and Baruch, stood silently as they watched the dock disappear slowly into the background. Jacob held Isaac in one arm while hugging Dora close to him with the other, tears streaming down his cheeks. "We're on our way home," he said.

As the ship moved slowly forward toward the Black Sea, those aboard were filled with renewed hope. Outside the infirmary, the doctor and a volunteer nurse covered the body of an elderly woman with a makeshift shroud of canvas. She had died before dawn and before realizing her dream of freedom. She would be buried at sea along with the man who lay on the bench beside her.

The ship was gliding through a calm sea under a bright blue sky. It was time now to give the dead their burial. Benny made his way to find the rabbi, who would hold a Kaddish.

A solemn mood descended among the refugees now as they said a final goodbye to those who had begun this journey with them. Their deaths tore at the very soul of who these refugees were. They had lost a brother and sister, a part of their family. As the rabbi prayed a prayer for the dead, Baruch and Shlomo gently lifted the bench where the two lay. They carried it to the side of the ship, where each body was allowed to slip slowly and silently from its resting place into the deep waters.

Being on the open sea helped the passengers to overcome the sadness they had felt after seeing the two people being buried. It also gave everyone a sense of freedom for the first time in months.

Jacob, holding tight to Isaac, made his way through those close to the side railing of the ship, so that the little boy could see the dolphins that were swimming alongside. People lifted their faces toward the sun, into the fresh sea breeze. Standing in silence, they took the salt air into their lungs. It was as if they could breathe for the first time.

Benny stood beside Baruch and Shlomo without talking, each looking out at the sea, deep in their own thoughts. They knew this was not going to be a journey without problems, but now there was hope for these people, and hope was what they needed.

The captain ordered the Turkish flag to be raised as the ship lowered its speed to enter the Bosphorus Strait. The vessel dropped anchor a few hundred yards from the shore of Istanbul. Residents of the city became aware of the ship and its cargo very quickly. During the night, refugees aboard the *Atlantic* could hear celebrations taking place among the large Jewish population ashore. Hearing the joy and shared celebration lifted the spirits of those on board. It reminded them of what was to be their future.

The next day was the festival of Yom Kippur, the Day of Atonement. The Jewish residents of Istanbul brought gifts of loaves and wine, along with fresh fruits and various provisions for the ship's passengers. They offered to mail letters for those who wanted to write to loved ones. Benny and Baruch, along with Rivka and Shlomo, made certain these gifts ended up where they were supposed to be.

Benny had not allowed himself to even think of reaching out to Varda since leaving Palestine. He knew that it would make what he had volunteered to do more difficult. He was aware that his commitment, along with that of the other volunteers, had to be 100 percent. However, now that reaching Palestine was on the horizon and the mission was almost accomplished, he felt he could expose that vulnerable part of himself to the pain of missing her. He decided to write a letter to Varda.

Benny's Letter to Varda

Varda, my love,

It has been well over a year since we said goodbye. The time away from you has been an eternity. We had no idea how long it would be, only that it had to be.

Writing has not been possible because of our situation. Now that we are close to completing this mission, I can reach out to you.

The memory of you these past months has kept my soul alive. I miss you, my love. I miss the beauty of your smile and the feel of your hand in mine. I miss you being next to me. I pray for the day we are together again.

If I am unable to write, and that's possible, remember my love for you.

Always,
Benny

Meanwhile, arguments ensued regarding taking on coal, food, and fresh water. Benny intervened, arguing that these had all been paid for in advance. He later told Shlomo, "It's like bargaining for your life with a bunch of pirates." Benny was getting used to the back-and-forth discussions about money with Spiro.

The food and fresh water were eventually delivered, but Benny was told there was a shortage of coal and there was none to be provided unless they paid cash. There was no choice but to pay the ransom for coal so they could leave port.

The Turkish pilot boat guided the *Atlantic* until it sailed into the Mediterranean, with calm seas ahead. Those on board welcomed the view of the open water. Relaxing in the salty sea air lifted the spirits of everyone able to take advantage of it.

Terror at Sea

Without warning, a violent storm formed, catching everyone onboard, including the captain, off guard. Dark monster-like clouds enveloped the ship. Flashes of lightning outlined the hundreds of refugees on deck. Giant waves tossed the ship back and forth without mercy as it creaked and moaned under the stress. The vessel keeled sideways, threatening to take on water, off balance because of the number of people aboard. Weight in the center of the ship would have to be shifted in order for it to stay afloat.

The captain shouted orders to the crew and to passengers below through a bullhorn from the bridge.

"Run starboard!"

"Run forward!"

Terrified people ran back and forth, following the captain's orders while the ship was being tossed about from bow to stern. Every person was in a panic. They frantically tried to push their weight against the wind, falling onto the wet deck, hanging on to one another as waves threatened to wash them overboard. At the same time, the rain's piercing needles pelted them, stinging their eyes and making it impossible to see.

There was terror in every part of the ship. People were convinced they were about to die. There was uncontrolled vomiting as hundreds tried to keep their balance, only to slip and fall into their own vomit. Screaming and chaos was everywhere as bodies were being tossed like ragdolls by the violent motion of the ship, leaving some bodies crushed together in pain, and others lifeless against the side panels of the passageways.

Then as quickly as it had begun, it was over.

Benny, Shlomo and Baruch met with some of the young passengers the next morning. It would be necessary for them to check on everyone and see how much damage had been done, then report back. The stronger of the young men were asked to go below and carry up all of the straw mattresses; they would hopefully dry out and could be used. Others who were physically able would fill buckets with seawater to scrub up the vomit and whatever else needed to be cleaned up.

Young and old alike huddled together against the walls of the passageways. Their faces were haggard and dirty, their hair still wet and matted against their scalps. Benny's own body remained soaked under his shirt and pants. Moving among the people, he could feel the salt from the seawater in his shoes. His voice was barely a whisper as if he were talking to himself: "We're alive. We survived."

He reached out to give a reassuring pat on the shoulder or head of those closest to him as he walked by. Some moaned as he approached, while others cried openly in discomfort; yet others remained silent, their eyes closed. He knew these people had been traumatized physically and emotionally and he felt helpless.

Benny Meets Eli

Benny stopped when he saw a frail-looking man crawling in circles on the floor in front of him. The man looked to be well over 80 and was behaving in a confused way, in a panic.

Benny leaned down and grasped the man's shoulder.

"Are you all right?" he asked gently. "Can I help you?"

The frenzied man ignored the question, continuing to crawl about, feeling around on the floor in front of him.

Benny asked again, this time a bit louder, "Can I help you? What are you looking for? Did you lose something?"

The man stopped what he was doing, got off his knees and turned, looking up at Benny. He began to cry and talk at the same time, speaking in Yiddish.

It was hard for Benny to make out his words between the sobs. He sat down on the floor beside the frail man. "Take a deep breath now and tell me: Are you alone on the ship?"

The man answered between sobs. It was still difficult to understand him.

"No . . . No, my wife Hannah is somewhere, I don't know where. I was sick. I threw up. I lost my teeth. I can't find my teeth." He started crying again.

Benny put his arm around the man's shoulder in an effort to reassure him.

"We're going to find your teeth—they have to be somewhere around here. And after we find your teeth, we're going to find your wife."

Benny got to his feet, helping the man to stand. He leaned down. "What's your name?"

"Eli," the man answered. "My name is Eli."

Benny put an arm around his shoulder. "Well, Eli, we're going to need a little help to find those teeth, so we are going to ask for help from all these people."

He hoped everyone would hear him as he shouted: "Listen, everyone! Our friend Eli here lost his teeth during the storm and needs our help to find them. All of you, please look on the floor around you!"

He spoke in German first, then Yiddish, repeating it in Czech. His loud voice could be heard up and down the passageway.

There was an immediate search for the teeth.

After a few moments, a weak voice down the passageway called out, "Here they are! I found them."

There were cheers as Benny made his way through the packed bodies to the place where the voice had come from. An older woman handed him the teeth.

Benny thanked her: "You did a great *mitzvah* today."

Her frail hand clung to his for a brief moment before letting go.

Benny returned to where he had left Eli. He smiled as he handed the old man the teeth: "You might want to wash these before putting them in your mouth."

He put his arm around Eli's shoulders again. "Now, come with me. Let's go find Hannah. You two need to stay together, right?"

Eli smiled a toothless grin, putting the teeth into his pocket. "Yes, let's find Hannah."

There was a certain amount of organized cooperation among those aboard ship, thanks to Rivka and Baruch's continued daily briefings with Shlomo and some of the group of young people from Osik. The straw mattresses that were brought up from below were used to sleep on at night and rolled up during the day, creating makeshift seats to sit on and allowing refugees to pick themselves up off the deck and share space with others. This simple act of cooperation seemed to lift spirits.

Day-to-day health conditions continued to worsen, however, due to having no sanitation and the lack of clean water. Diarrhea, developing into dysentery, and overall malnourishment was taking its toll, especially among older people. Deaths and daily burials were becoming more common.

Meanwhile the *Atlantic* was traveling at a slower speed on its way to Crete, stopping frequently off the Dodecanese Islands, which belonged to Italy, an ally of Germany. Spiro and his crew were acting in a curiously nervous fashion. They would anchor in a cove behind an island during the day, and pull anchor to sail at night.

Finally, they arrived at the port of Heraklion on the coast of Crete. The *Atlantic* was forced to dock initially at the pier because the port authorities, aware of the condition of the passengers aboard, would not let the ship enter the harbor. The sight of this strange-looking vessel with a Panamanian flag that had docked by the pier in the middle of the night caused curiosity among the local people. Rumors spread quickly, including word about Jewish refugees on their way to Palestine who were sick and in dire need.

Two representatives from the Jewish community of Crete obtained permission to board the ship. They met with Benny and Baruch, offering their assistance. They were shocked, not only at the living conditions the refugees were forced to survive in, but also at the condition of the refugees themselves.

Captain Spiro made an awkward attempt to find excuses for the situation, telling the Jewish representatives that he was powerless. He complained about lack of supplies, including coal. They listened politely, then offered to mediate for the refugees between him and the port authorities, an idea which he eagerly accepted.

Benny and Baruch knew what Spiro was up to again. They thanked the two men, who said goodbye, offering their handshake along with a promise of returning.

Within days, fresh food, including fruits and vegetables, arrived. This would allow Rivka to continue to feed those who so desperately needed it. The Jewish community had also managed to raise enough money to purchase fresh water and coal, which hopefully would allow the voyage to continue.

Captain Spiro continued making excuses for why he could not raise anchor and set sail. Benny became more and more suspicious and decided to form a small, select and discreet group to keep an eye on Spiro, along with those crew members who were a part of his little band of thieves. Their behavior made it more and more obvious that Spiro was up to no good.

Meanwhile the negotiations for promised coal failed, according to Spiro. The coal had arrived—but not enough to get the ship to Palestine. The frustration and mistrust of Spiro among Benny and the others grew with each day.

War Breaks Out

News of Italy's declaration of war against Greece came as a surprise to everyone aboard ship. The *Atlantic* was now docked at a pier in a country that was at war with Germany. The captain at once ordered the crew to paint the hull of the ship with neutral Panamanian colors. There was visible panic among the entire crew whenever threatening airplanes flew overhead.

The refugees were too weak to react. They believed nothing was going to change. They were still trapped on a ship going nowhere, still sick, thirsty, and hungry. Day after day, they had to witness loved ones among them die and not be given a burial because they were not at sea. Many saw this ship now, not as a ship of freedom, but a ship of the dead.

The island authorities began insisting to Captain Spiro that the ship could no longer remain docked. Provisions had to be loaded with no more delays and the *Atlantic* had to set sail. Spiro argued with them, but his reasons were ignored.

Benny and those chosen to watch the captain and crew were aware that Spiro was close to being out of control. He was almost hysterical, shouting at everyone while coal was being loaded.

The next day, Baruch and Benny said goodbye to the representatives of the Jewish community after thanking them for their generosity. The *Atlantic* then pulled away from the dock late at night. However, instead of heading out to sea, the captain followed the coastline of Crete, taking the ship into a cove for the night.

The next morning, before sunrise, those watching the captain managed to overpower him, along with some of the crew members who were in lifebelts about to abandon ship. They allowed the crew members to escape but held on to the captain. They dragged the struggling Spiro to the captain's cabin where they waited with him until Benny arrived.

Benny spoke with Spiro at length, questioning him before deciding to constrain him under the watch of a volunteer. He would be locked in his cabin until they were well underway at sea.

Everyone aboard was aware of the struggle that had taken place, and rumors spread very quickly about some of the missing crew and the ship's captain being locked up in his own cabin. Strangely enough, instead of creating fear among those aboard, these rumors lifted people's spirits.

One of the refugees approached Benny, introducing himself as Max. Speaking in Czech, he offered his expertise as an engineer to help command the ship since it was obvious the captain could not be trusted. He informed Benny of others on board who were strong and in reasonably healthy condition and more than willing to help get the ship to Palestine.

Benny thanked him and asked that he bring those capable and willing to the captain's bridge to meet with him, along with Baruch and Shlomo.

"We will all take part in a plan to get this ship moving," he said with determination.

Later, the number of volunteers coming forward to do whatever was necessary was uplifting. Benny remained on the bridge with Shlomo and Baruch after they had all left.

"You know what?" he smiled. "I think we're going to be all right."

They agreed.

The crew whose job it was to fire the ship's engines and maintain the engine room said that it was impossible to get enough pressure built up in the boiler to get the ship moving.

Benny didn't hesitate. He turned to the Czech engineer: "Max, let's get that crew out of the engine room. We'll replace them with volunteers. These men will sabotage us any way they can."

Max agreed. He passed on the message to Karl, a man whom he had already chosen to be his second-in-command, and the two of them replaced the crew with willing and capable volunteers. The Greek crew members went to their quarters without arguments or any response, other than smug grins they didn't bother to hide.

The volunteers got the ship moving. But before long, they discovered there was very little coal left in the stokehole. After talking to some of the passengers, Benny realized what the captain and some of his crew had been up to the night before they tried to abandon ship. They had dumped all the good coal, purchased earlier, into the sea.

Desperate Measures

Benny once again called an emergency meeting between those in charge. His words were somber.

"We do not have enough coal to get us to Palestine," he began. "In fact there is not enough coal to get us to Cyprus, even if we wanted to do that. Since it's a British port, this ship could be immediately seized for transporting illegal immigrants. We are currently without power and practically drifting."

Benny showed a determination he didn't necessarily believe:

"We must take desperate measures to keep us moving."

It didn't take long before they knew what those desperate measures were. Everyone on board who was strong, healthy and able was to take part in collecting wood that could be used as fuel. Jacob explained to Dora the urgency of the situation. It was time for him to join those trying to save the ship, which meant leaving her and Isaac with the other mothers and their children.

When Baruch saw Jacob, he shook his hand, slapping him on the shoulder.

"Good to have you, Jacob. Let's create some fuel, shall we?"

The young man laughed. It felt good to be with his friend again.

A few of the ship's crew members who wanted no part of the captain's plot offered to help. They found the necessary tools and willingly took part in dismantling their quarters. Shlomo oversaw the stripping of paneling from walls, along with the removal of doors. Everything would be cut up and put into the stokehole. Anything made of wood was going to become fuel. The crew offered to take down one of the ship's masts. Benny thanked them and accepted the offer. Baruch ordered the dismantling and removal of every makeshift bed below, leaving those who had been willing to sleep there, even in the horrendous conditions, without beds. The galley was not touched, as Rivka still had to feed people.

When the exhausted group finished, what once looked like a ship was now a shell. Refugees would now share open space with those who had died. The bodies that had been laid out on benches awaiting burial at sea lay on the deck, covered with makeshift tarps.

Benny decided to pay Captain Spiro a visit. He knew the captain couldn't help but see what was going on as he watched from his cabin.

When Benny entered the locked cabin, Spiro actually seemed

glad to see him. Benny sat down on a chair next to the bunk where he was lying. He looked around the captain's cabin.

"We will probably have to take some of this furniture," he stated. "It will make things a bit more uncomfortable for you, but I'm sure you can understand." His comment was filled with sarcasm.

Spiro sat up on the bunk and put his head down in his hands. Both men sat in silence for a few minutes. Spiro was the first to speak.

"I'm sorry." He looked sincere to Benny as he continued: "I didn't want to captain this ship, but I had no choice."

Benny listened as he talked, relating the stories they had already heard about Jewish refugees and the chances of such ships making it to Palestine. Spiro told him that after seeing the conditions of the ship he was convinced it would not make the voyage; then there was his real fear of being imprisoned by the British.

While Spiro spoke, Benny could see that he was being genuine. The two men sat in silence again before Benny responded.

"What you've told me may all be true, Spiro, but what you and your men did was criminal and deserved imprisonment. You and your crew were no more than a band of the worst kind of thieves. You lied and manipulated and you stole from good people who had already gone through a living hell. You created situations that possibly contributed to the death of good people, and then finally you tried to abandon your command like rats, leaving all of us to sink into the sea."

The more Benny spoke, the more his anger grew, and he had the urge to lift Spiro off the bunk he was sitting on and throw him into the cabin wall.

Spiro saw the anger and contempt on Benny's face. He accepted the angry words, along with his contempt.

"I don't expect you to forgive me," he replied, "but I can help you if you will let me. You are using some of the crew, so give me a chance too."

Benny saw that the captain was being sincere. He was quiet for a moment before answering.

"All right, but there are good people who will be watching you at all times. God help you if you try anything."

There was a possibility that Benny was making a mistake, but Max and Karl might need the captain's experience as they got closer to Palestine.

Spiro showed his gratitude, along with his humility, by attempting to give Benny an awkward hug.

Benny shrugged the attempt off. "Let's go introduce you to Max and Karl."

The ship was now making its way slowly. Those aboard could see nothing but an expanse of open sea.

The following days were somber ones, filled with prayers as those who had died were given their burial at sea. Following the final service, another prayer was said: "May these tarps that have covered our brothers and sisters never be used again."

The British

Fuel was again running low. The sea remained calm, which was fortunate as the *Atlantic* struggled to maintain any speed at all. Captain Spiro was cooperating well with Max and Karl.

One day, what appeared to be warships on the horizon were spotted by the captain. He was correct: the two ships were British destroyers. Before long the *Atlantic* was receiving Morse code messages demanding to know where the ship and its passengers were headed. The captain's knowledge, along with his ability to come up with quick answers, seemed to satisfy the British. He even asked if they could spare some fuel, telling them that fuel was running out, but they declined, offering no assistance.

The two ships continued following the *Atlantic* slowly alongside, but made no further contact. Finally, they increased their speed and disappeared.

Land was sighted on the horizon the next day. According to navigation maps, it appeared to be Cyprus, which meant they were in British territory. Captain Spiro was showing signs of being nervous again. Max and Karl voiced their own concerns but agreed that at least they were under the protection of the British. They all knew that without fuel they would not be able to continue.

It wasn't too long before a small boat flying a British flag was spotted by those aboard. It appeared to be heading toward the ship. The refugees were instantly gripped by the fear of what was going to happen to them because of the strict laws on immigration to Palestine.

Captain Spiro and his crew joined those aboard in their fear of the British. Spiro approached Benny: "Let's tell them we're headed for Port Said in Egypt."

Benny ignored the suggestion. "No, we're going to tell them the truth, that we're on our way to Haifa."

The small boat pulled alongside, allowing a British officer to board the *Atlantic*.

Benny approached the officer smiling, his hand extended to shake the man's hand. It was ignored. Benny chose not to let the cold response bother him and explained they were on their way to the port of Haifa, but fuel had run out, leaving them in need of assistance.

The officer maintained his aloofness as he listened, then with no further explanation ordered the *Atlantic* to be towed by British naval police to Limassol, Cyprus.

The ship was anchored outside of Limassol harbor. When British officers saw the condition of those aboard, they were horrified. They ordered the removal of some of the passengers to a hospital in Limassol, which meant they would have to remain in Cyprus after the ship sailed. Benny didn't like the idea of leaving anyone behind but told himself they were actually better off. They were safe and would not have to face more suffering on a ship with an uncertain destination.

Again, the local Jewish community would come to the rescue of the immigrants aboard the *Atlantic*. News of the anchored ship with its refugees on the way to Palestine spread quickly among the Jewish residents of Limassol. One of the local doctors at the hospital asked for donations to provide food and fuel so that the ship could continue its voyage to Palestine. The money was taken to the office of British naval operations where it was accepted by a clerk whose expression was very much as if he were validating something that had a bad smell to it. The funds being provided for fuel, as well as food and water, created a problem for the British. Now they would be forced to make a decision about what exactly to do with these people. The decision was made to place British military aboard and sail this unfortunate cargo of immigrants to Haifa.

Members of the British military boarded the *Atlantic* before lifting anchor. They pushed their way onto the deck, using unnecessary force to crowd between older refugees too weak and too afraid to object. Baruch, along with Shlomo and Jacob, made certain that the younger immigrants guided the most vulnerable of these older passengers to a place where they would not be injured. Hundreds were gathering on the deck now, excited at the realization that they were on their way to see their families.

Benny made his way to find Captain Spiro. He asked that he follow him, away from Max and Karl. When they were in private, he explained to him that the British military would be escorting the ship to Haifa and that the outcome once there was unknown.

Spiro nodded, acknowledging that he understood.

Benny continued: "We will be lifting anchor in the morning to leave Cyprus for Haifa. I want you to get your crew and I want you to quietly get off the ship tonight. None of us will try to stop you. You will have to be careful of the British, though, because they will be standing guard. You understand that if you are caught, I won't be able to help you."

Spiro grabbed Benny's hand.

"Thank you, my friend," he said gratefully. "God be with you."

Benny slapped Spiro's shoulder. "*Mazel tov. Shalom.*"

Benny watched Spiro as he hurriedly left to find his crew, and repeated to himself, "*Mazel tov.* We're all going to need it." Then he returned to join Max and Karl.

The next morning the number of British sailors on board was reinforced. An officer approached Benny: "Where is your captain? And I don't see a crew. Where is the crew that mans this ship?"

Benny answered politely, "This is it. We are all there is. The captain along with his crew abandoned ship some time ago. We've been doing the best we can to navigate. You can see we've had to take desperate measures because we ran out of fuel."

The officer remained aloof. "Yes, I can see. A grim situation indeed. Well, the Royal Navy will be escorting you to Haifa."

He left without saying another word.

The realization that the *Atlantic* would reach the port of Haifa in just 24 hours lifted the spirits of everyone, including those who were most frail. Finally, they would arrive in Eretz Israel and they would be home.

The Arrival

Before daybreak the next day, all the refugees who were able to stand gathered on deck, wherever there was space, to watch as the *Atlantic* moved slowly toward Mount Carmel.

Once the mountain was in view, spontaneous singing broke out, softly at first, then louder. Tears streamed unashamedly down the faces of young and old alike, with sobs mixed among the words, as they began to sing "Hatikva."

As the *Atlantic* anchored outside the harbor, those on board recognized the two empty ships that had left before them, carrying immigrants from Bratislava. There was also a large passenger liner with three smoke stacks anchored nearby. A British plane was very noticeable as it circled above.

Before long, Palestinian police officers, including a small Jewish delegation, boarded the ship, asking to meet with the captain. The purpose of the meeting became known very quickly. Everyone on board the *Atlantic* was to be transferred immediately to another ship. Benny questioned the Jewish delegation. The explanation given for why they were going to be transferred to another ship—for quarantine—didn't make sense to him.

Benny tried to explain: "Those aboard have been through months of torturous conditions, along with starvation, and are in fragile condition. To make them pack up and relocate now to another ship would be inhumane."

He hoped that even if the Palestinian police didn't listen, those in the Jewish delegation would.

He continued with a final plea: "These people have suffered

unimaginable tortures on this ship. They have been taken advantage of by unscrupulous people who robbed them of their possessions in order to survive. They were deprived of everything any human being should have for survival. They have watched, helpless, as their brothers and sisters became ill and died. They shared what little space they had with the dead and they have endured because of who they are.

"This ship, with all its terror, became a familiar place and, as strange as it may seem to you, it is a part of their survival. Now, when they have come to what they believe is the end of their treacherous journey, about to find their place in the land they dreamed of, the land we all love . . . when you tell them they have to board another ship into the unknown, it will do what nothing else could do. It will destroy them. I beg you as a Jew, as a human being, do not do this."

Benny's voice was hoarse with emotion. He had said all he could. Would it help? He didn't know.

The next morning, government employees of the British boarded the ship. They announced that the refugees should make available to them all of their belongings to be searched. Making their way throughout the ship, the officials systematically went through every item, removing whatever they chose. There was total confusion among the refugees as they watched their belongings being ripped from their suitcases and bags. Photos and letters were thrown about like trash.

Benny approached those he thought were in charge, only to be told: "They have their orders."

There was nothing anyone could do. It was obvious to him that the British were not going to let those aboard the *Atlantic* have an easy time of it.

Orders to Leave

There was no disputing the orders for the passengers of the *Atlantic* to disembark. Benny, along with the others, watched as police boats circled the ship. Before dawn the first group, consisting mostly of women and children, were loaded onto waiting launches. It was agreed that Baruch and Rivka, along with Benny, would remain on the ship until all transfers from the *Atlantic* to another ship, the *Patria*, were complete.

Shlomo offered to go with the first group, taking with him three of the young refugee volunteers. The logic was to try to oversee some organization and give comfort, if possible. Benny watched as his friend got onto the second launch and headed toward the passenger ship. Patrol boats, along with a British plane circling low above the ship, made sure that no refugee would escape as they made their way to the launches.

Later in the morning, Jacob and Dora, with Isaac, were loaded onto the third boat, along with others who had children. Those on deck watched as they waited for their turn. They were finally going to leave this ship of death and suffering.

As the launch left the side of the *Atlantic*, the occupants of the boat could see the huge gray passenger ship in the distance. It looked ominous to Jacob. He tightened his hold on Isaac, clasping the hand of Dora. He was overcome with a feeling of danger. Waves were causing the launch to move slowly. It was going to take longer for them to reach the *Patria* than the others. Jacob considered the distance between them and the ship where they were to be imprisoned again to be about 250 yards.

Sinking of the Patria

The terrifying sound of an explosion shocked Jacob and those aboard the small boat. They were even more stunned by the sight of the huge passenger ship leaning to one side, before disappearing within minutes beneath the water. The launch was far enough away to avoid being sucked down as the great ship sank. Lifeless, torn bodies from the explosion were thrown into the water. Other people were shouting for help as they fought to survive by grabbing onto pieces of debris and one another in a sea of blood. Images of the horror would last in the minds of those who survived for ever.

What no one on the *Atlantic* knew was that the British had no intentions of allowing those aboard the ship to ever set foot on land. Land curfews had been enacted before the ship arrived so that there could be no communication between passengers on the *Atlantic* and anyone in Palestine. British plans were to immediately transfer immigrants, upon arrival, to other ships for deportation to one of the British colonies.

After news emerged of the British plan to deport all the refugees aboard the *Atlantic*, as well as the passengers of the other two ships that had arrived earlier, representatives of the Jewish Agency, along with others from various Jewish organizations, had tried to negotiate with British representatives of the king, but without success. They realized the quarantine aboard the *Patria* was just an excuse. Once again, these immigrants were to become nothing more than a cargo, shipped to another place, rumored to be the British colony Mauritius. After failing in their efforts, the delegates from the Jewish community accepted the inevitable; however, the Haganah did not. There was also another plan, and this one was being carefully put together by the Haganah. Its leaders would make their own secret plans to delay the exportation of hundreds of Jews from what was rightfully their homeland.

The Failed Plan

Members of the Haganah would board the *Patria* as maintenance crews. Once aboard, a small bomb would be planted in the engine room, attached to the inside wall; when detonated, it would blow a small hole in the side of the ship, making just enough damage to cause a leak that would need to be repaired before the ship could sail. This would give more time for further negotiations.

Dressed in maintenance uniforms, the men of the Haganah would announce it was necessary to evacuate the areas for cleaning and disinfecting. Everyone, without exception, would be ordered to gather on deck by 8:00 AM the next morning. These orders were designed to make certain that those in the endangered area would be safe. To the horror of everyone on the *Atlantic*, and in Haifa, the plan failed. The residents of Haifa, as well as the passengers on the *Atlantic*, watched helplessly, in shock, while rescue operations began to save as many victims as possible. Some of those blown free of the *Patria* were able to swim to a jetty in the harbor and were picked up immediately by British police. Others continued to cling to pieces of wreckage, waiting to be picked up by the port authorities. Lifeboats from ships anchored in the harbor were lowered into the sea to help rescue as many as possible.

Cold, wet, and in shock, the survivors were brought ashore. Those who could stand or walk did so, while others were carried on stretchers. Temporary care was given to those who were bleeding. The area was being guarded by British police to ensure that nobody from the local Jewish community would interfere and no survivor would escape. At the same time, the British quickly came up with a solution for dealing with those being brought ashore. They would be taken to a warehouse where they would be confined until they could be relocated along with the other refugees.

The very next day, the *Atlantic* was towed into Haifa harbor and disembarkation began. A constant downpour of rain made the deck slippery and dangerous for the older refugees, who were trying to carry what few belongings they had. Under the direction of Baruch and Rivka, the young guided those who needed help.

Because there were so many who were weakened by dysentery, along with other illnesses, the process was slow, which irritated the officers in charge of the operation. Their shouts of "Hurry!" and "Move along now!" only caused more anxiety and confusion among those who were already distraught at what they had witnessed.

Benny approached the officer in charge.

"Look," he said, "I understand you're doing your job, but can't you have your officers be a little more patient with the older people?"

The man stared at Benny coldly, hesitated, then told one of the officers, "Tell them to take it a bit easier on the old ones."

Benny's "thank you" was ignored.

The removal of refugees would take days, continuing at a slow pace. Those left on the ship while waiting to disembark found themselves with space to move about for the first time in months since boarding the *Atlantic*. They could now see the skeletal remains of this vessel, where starvation and suffering could only be mercifully dealt with by death, leaving the pain of loss behind. Even though they didn't know where they were going, touching their feet on land would be a blessing.

Police guards watched closely so there could be no possible communication by refugees leaving the ship as they were boarded onto waiting buses. Once on the buses, they were taken to a disinfecting center.

British workers ordered each group as they arrived to undress. After removing their clothing, people were left to stand naked while their clothes were gathered up and put into ovens to be disinfected. When the order finally came to enter the showers, they were grateful. Some of the old and weak simply sat on the floor, letting the water pour over them, until helped to their feet. Afterwards, still wet from the shower, people were handed back their clothes. Even though they were still damp, everyone appreciated the fact that they were clean and their bodies covered again.

Then the command came to "line up to be vaccinated."

Next came the armed police, who surrounded the buses while they were reboarded. These refugees would be taken to Atlit, a few miles from Haifa, where they would join others taken there previously.

The camp at Atlit looked formidable. It was set on a large field surrounded by barbed wire. There were approximately a hundred barracks, including tents. Areas were divided into sections, also enclosed by barbed wire. The men's barracks were in a different section from the women's and children's. Survivors from the *Patria* had been separated from refugees from the *Atlantic* for some unknown reason. The barbed-wire fences keeping them apart were higher and insurmountable. Guards were made up of both British police and Jewish auxiliary police.

Refugees were assigned specific barracks. Blankets, pots and pans, along with other essential articles, were distributed eventually. After all they had gone through these past months on the *Atlantic*, and the rough humiliation before arriving here at the camp in Atlit, the refugees actually appreciated settling in. The only question now was: "How long will this last?"

Benny walked around outside the barracks. He had shared in

the experience of those immigrants involved in the disembarkation of the *Atlantic*, and the inhumane treatment during the disinfecting process, and this had left him even more connected to these people. He was no longer someone who was there to oversee and shepherd them; he was one of them.

He stood looking at the high barbed-wire fence separating the survivors of the *Patria* from the refugees on the *Atlantic*. The thought occurred to him: *There must be some decision being argued out about what to do with those aboard the* Patria. He knew the *Patria* had been sabotaged, but did the British think someone on board was guilty or was this just another political scheme at a higher level?

A major concern for him was Shlomo. Since it was impossible to talk with anyone, how could he find out if his friend was okay? Was he injured? Was he alive?

Benny continued to stand beside the fence until the penetrating night air made it necessary to return to the barracks.

The Visitor

By the next morning, things had started to settle down for everyone. Someone had made tea and set out biscuits that had been provided, along with other food supplies. Conversations were going on between some of the people.

Benny was aware of how quickly those in the barracks had adjusted to their new surroundings. Taking a cup of tea and a biscuit, he went outside into the camp yard. He liked feeling the crisp morning air. While standing there, he saw at a distance the appearance of a tall man, with what looked like a file of papers in his hand, walking toward the barracks, accompanied by a guard. Taking another drink of his tea, he continued to watch as the two men came closer. The tall one looked vaguely familiar. As they got closer, he realized who it was. Benny's immediate reaction was to say his name aloud in disbelief: "Zev Ronen!"

The guard made certain everything was correct by checking the papers in the file Zev had brought. Once satisfied that everything matched and the connection between Zev and Benny had been completed, the guard left.

Benny grabbed Zev's hand. "How did you find me?" he asked. "How did you know I was here?"

Zev laughed, slapping Benny on the shoulder. "You didn't think we would abandon you, did you?"

"No," Benny answered, "but how did you know I was here?"

Zev became serious. "Shlomo contacted us," he explained. "He told us you were being taken to Atlit."

When Benny heard this, he exhaled a deep sigh of relief. "Thank God. I didn't know if he had survived the sinking of the *Patria*."

He listened closely as Zev told him the details of how Shlomo had been blown off the ship and how he was able, even though injured, to swim to shore unnoticed.

Zev then went on to tell him about the arguments between the British authorities and the Jewish Agency regarding proof of citizenship for Benny and the other volunteers.

"The British are hard to deal with regarding immigration of Jews into Israel," he explained. "They don't want the Arab community upset and they also think there could be a possibility of German spies among the Jews. It's hard to convince them otherwise. The sinking of the *Patria* was definitely sabotage and they suspect everyone."

"What are they going to do with these poor refugees?" Benny asked. "They've been through the tortures of hell."

He didn't like to hear Zev's answer.

"Those on the *Atlantic* will be deported to Mauritius, most likely right away. We can't stop that. They're considered to be illegal immigrants. The survivors from the *Patria* will be allowed to stay in Israel. The British will declare an act of humane clemency because there were so many who died when the *Patria* sank, and because of the trauma to those who managed to survive.

"Rivka and you will leave here with me today and, as you are now aware, Shlomo is already back. I'm going over to the women's barracks now to see Rivka. I'll bring her back with me; then we will be able to leave for Haifa."

Zev's appearance and the information he had shared came as a total surprise to Benny, and he had to process everything quickly. He would have to say goodbye to Jacob and Dora. The thought of them being deported to Mauritius with little Isaac was not something he wanted to accept, yet he knew it was out of his control.

He found Jacob in one of the barracks. It would be difficult to say goodbye, especially because of what he had to tell him about the future that lay ahead for everyone. He realized it would be best if he heard the news from him.

Jacob remained quiet as he listened. Benny told him that everyone on the *Atlantic* was about to be transferred to Mauritius. He explained how they had no power to overcome the British government, basically telling him that Eretz Israel, as it stood that day, was helpless.

Benny's words came from the heart.

"Jacob, I will give you some helpful advice that I want you to take in order to make life easier for you and your family. Do not resist this decision by the British; you cannot win. Think only of yourself, Dora, and little Isaac. Don't think that you will be forgotten. That will not happen. You will return, I promise. Look at Mauritius as your last stop before coming home."

He could tell that Jacob had heard every word. He hugged the younger man, and the two shook hands.

Benny's final words before leaving were: "I'm sorry." As he walked away, his chest was heavy with emotion. He felt as if he were deserting a friend.

Walking through the barracks as he left, Benny looked around at the refugees who had endured so much to get here. He could only hope that Mauritius would be their final stop before the Israeli government could bring them home. Taking his suitcase from under the cot, he went outside to wait for Zev to return.

When Zev turned up without Rivka, Benny was surprised. Zev's explanation surprised him even more. He told Benny, "It seems that Rivka wants to remain with the refugees and go to Mauritius. She and someone whose name is Baruch are a couple. How they met in Osik and have worked together this entire time is quite a story. I'm guessing they will be taking advantage of the rabbi when they get to Mauritius."

Benny grinned, shaking his head. "Well, that is something I did not know. She's a strong woman and he's a good man. I guess there's some good in everything."

Zev waved to the guard to come over and escort them through the gate. He slapped Benny on the back: "Come on, there are some people waiting to meet you in Haifa."

After Benny said goodbye to Jacob, rumors of impending deportation moved very quickly throughout the camp, causing even more distress among the refugees. Their anger and unrest grew as they asked, "Why aren't the Jews fighting for us?"

There was talk about a rebellion among the younger people if the British tried to relocate them to another camp. The rumor about being transported to a British colony somewhere thousands of miles away from their homeland was unthinkable. Were they animals to be shipped wherever the British decided? Were they expected to follow like sheep with no resistance? The answer for them was: "Not without a fight."

Jewish organizations were aware of the previous arrival of two large Dutch steamships anchored in the Haifa harbor. Organized strikes and protests were already causing unrest on the streets. British security was tightened around the harbor, and curfews were being strictly enforced. Guards armed with machine guns, along with police carrying clubs, walked the streets of Haifa. As rumors about being deported spread throughout the detention camp, plans to remove the refugees had already been put into play.

The Deportation Begins

The announcement came shortly after dinner to prepare for deportation the next morning. There was no explanation other than "It's time to continue your voyage." After the announcement, the door to each barrack was locked so that no one could go outside. The usual Palestinian police officers who stood guard at night were relieved of their duties and replaced by British guards. The entire camp was surrounded by British soldiers. Machine-gun posts were set up at each corner of the enclosure.

Armed guards with bayonets moved into the camp soon after dark, along with Palestinian police. Throughout the night, buses and trucks began arriving that would be used to transport the refugees to the harbor, where they would be loaded onto the waiting ships after processing.

Just before dawn, each barracks was entered simultaneously by guards armed with guns and clubs, accompanied by dogs. What happened next was played out in every barracks.

The order to assemble and prepare to embark was given. When

no one moved, the command to attack was given. Dogs barked viciously, baring their teeth, but were held back by their handlers, to be turned loose if necessary. Refugees were thrown from their beds onto the floor, kicking and screaming. Some of the younger men were clubbed over the head; when they fell, they were kicked and dragged out to be handed over to guards waiting outside. Here they were beaten again and immediately thrown into the back of trucks, which were also guarded by vicious dogs and their handlers.

Older refugees who saw what was happening fell to their knees, crying and pleading with the soldiers to "leave us here to die." With their pleas ignored, they were dragged bleeding, with flesh scraped from their fragile bodies, to be tossed like sacks of flour into the back of buses, where piles of refugees were accumulating very quickly. Women who tried to resist were beaten and dragged without mercy, treated no differently from the men.

Jacob recalled Benny's warning and remained calm. Still, he received one striking blow across his back, and another to his head, knocking him to the floor and rendering him semiconscious. He managed to walk to the truck, where he was shoved into the back along with other beaten and bloody bodies lying in helpless piles on the floor. One of the younger men lying next to Jacob was moaning, sobbing uncontrollably. Blood was running down his face. It looked to Jacob as if one of the young man's eyes was partially gone.

Jacob pulled the sobbing young man closer so that his head could rest across his knees. He rocked him as if he were comforting little Isaac. The shock of the cruelty in what he was witnessing was more painful than the blows he had received. He hoped Dora had sense enough not to resist along with the others.

Once the trucks were loaded, tarps were used to cover the refugees inside. The tarps were tightly fastened down so that those inside could not see out, nor could anyone see the living cargo inside. Buses accompanying the trucks were then loaded with British soldiers and guards. They followed the trucks to Haifa port where the broken bodies of unwanted Jewish refugees were to be offloaded and forcibly loaded onto two Dutch ships. These ships would remove them from the homeland they had so desperately dreamed of and take them to a prison camp on the island of Mauritius, governed by the British.

The convoy reached the port where the two Dutch ships were waiting. Once there, everyone who was able to get out of the trucks on their own was directed under guard to a warehouse-type building. Some who had to be carried on stretchers were dropped without any conscience onto the floor of the building, left to lie there until one of their own could help them. A few people with the worst injuries were transferred to the hospital; the young man whom Jacob had tried to comfort was one of them.

Every refugee was examined. Personal belongings, thrown onto the trucks with them, were gone through at port customs. Still weak and in shock, refugees watched without objecting as their belongings were boldly stolen by customs officers. What was not stolen was simply thrown onto the floor like trash. Hours later, civil servants, flanked by armed British guards, checked people's names against those on lists that had been provided by the British, and embarking could begin. Refugees were directed to a designated ship according to the names on the lists.

Jacob was getting worried. He had not been able to see Dora and little Isaac among those getting out of the trucks or those filing into the building for examination. He wasn't able to separate himself from his fellow refugees to search for them.

What if they were boarded onto the other ship? he thought, beginning to panic. He scanned the line behind him. Finally, he saw Isaac waving his small arms. Dora had lifted the child above her shoulders and was holding him while he waved.

Jacob shouted as loud as he could: "Dora, up here! I'm here!"

Finally, he knew that she had heard him. She lowered Isaac and waved. He could barely see her hand, but he knew she was waving to let him know they had found each other and thankfully would be on the same ship.

All refugees were directed below deck and would remain there until the ships were well out to sea; then they would be allowed to return to the decks if they wanted to. This was not going to be the torturous voyage it had been on the *Atlantic*. There was space to move around, and food provided by a polite Dutch crew. The weak and injured refugees, young and old alike, would now be able to gain healthier bodies. However, nothing would change the saddened and broken hearts of those aboard who had been expelled from their homeland to be shipped into the unknown.

12

REUNIONS AND FAREWELLS

The Meeting

When Zev and Benny got to the Haifa apartment, Shlomo was waiting to meet them as they entered.

As soon as Benny saw Shlomo he grabbed his friend and gave him a big hug, then stood back. He made a fist and punched him in the shoulder, then stood back again, smiling. "You made it, my friend, you made it."

It was obvious to those observing the interaction between these two men that there was a special bond of friendship between them.

Benny had not yet noticed the others in the adjoining room. It was Zev's turn now to interrupt.

"Shlomo has already been re-introduced, so Benny, let me re-introduce you to someone you've met before. I'm sure you remember David Ben-Gurion."

David got to his feet and shook hands with a surprised Benny, but he was not as surprised as when Zelda stood up to offer her hand.

She smiled, firmly taking his hand in hers. "It's wonderful to see you, Benny." She shook his hand, then sat down in the chair again, lighting a cigarette.

Zev continued: "Let's all sit down and get comfortable."

He focused first on Benny. "David and Zelda have come here to meet with you and Shlomo because they, along with myself, would like to hear about the past months. You can be as brief as you like. We know there is too much to retell. Your feedback while dealing with the British is important, however." He grinned. "We don't expect to hear everything tonight."

Zev now became serious again, aiming what he was going to say at both Benny and Shlomo. "We want to submit a plan to you both which involves your joining the leadership on a permanent basis. We know you are tired right now and we respect that, but we want you to consider our plan after you've taken some time off to recuperate from these past months."

Now it was David's turn to speak.

"We have booked hotel rooms for tonight," he began. "We want to remain in Haifa until the Dutch ships carrying our people have left the harbor. Security will be lightened after they have boarded. We're going to try to get onto the dock if we can, to see them leave. We'll see—maybe it won't be possible—but we are going to try."

Zelda interrupted David. "In the meantime," she said brightly, "we are going to buy you the best dinner at the finest restaurant in Haifa; then we'll talk some more. Okay, kids?"

Benny and Shlomo both nodded their heads, smiling. "How can we turn you down? A good meal sounds good. No, it sounds great!"

They all left the apartment and checked into the hotel that had been arranged for them by Zev.

Benny stood in the shower for a long time, letting the strong force of hot water pour over his head and run down his body, producing a feeling of relaxation he hadn't felt for many months.

Later, lying on the bed, he closed his eyes. He thought of Varda for the first time since arriving in Haifa. She was so close he could almost imagine their meeting. Saying her name into the darkness of the room, he whispered, "Tomorrow, tomorrow, my love. We'll be together." Then he fell into a deep sleep.

He was awakened by a persistent knocking on the hotel-room door that startled him. He had forgotten where he was.

Shlomo was in his usual good spirits: "Come on, my friend, let's go get some of that great food."

Benny laughed. "All right, let's do it. I'm hungry too. For once, I might eat more than you."

David and Zelda were waiting for them when they got to the lobby.

The dinner conversation was pleasant and the food was delicious. David ordered wine with dinner and, after dinner, cognac, which relaxed the mood of everyone. After the meal, Zelda suggested the four of them take a short walk back to the hotel to enjoy the night air.

When they reached the hotel, David invited everyone to his room to continue the discussion regarding Benny and Shlomo becoming a permanent part of the Jewish leadership organization.

The talks went on for hours. It was encouraged and agreed that both Benny and Shlomo would return to Yagur and take up their lives as before; however, they would have to maintain secrecy regarding their involvement within the organization. Before leaving David's room, everyone shook hands and arrangements were made to meet in the lobby at four o'clock in the morning. From the hotel, they would go to the harbor.

The Sad Farewell

It was not quite daylight when the group met outside the hotel. When they arrived at the harbor the sun was beginning to brighten, reflecting itself on the water. Palestinian security police were still walking the dock, but the trucks with guards had left. Once the refugees were boarded, the British had posted watch by each ship but relieved the soldiers of their duties.

Zev suggested that the four of them simply walk as if they had one specific destination in mind, without looking in any direction but straight ahead.

"Go to the end of the dock and stop," he instructed. "If the ships have left, it still takes them a while to get out of the harbor. We might be able to see them."

The dock workers were busy, and the security guards were talking among themselves, ignoring them as they passed. There was no security posted where the two Dutch ships had been loaded yesterday. It was evident that the vessels had left for sea as soon as everyone had embarked.

Disappointed and saddened to have missed seeing the ships, Zelda, who had been unusually quiet, spoke for the first time: "Well, perhaps it's just as well we didn't see the ships. Seeing them would have made us even more sad."

David agreed. His voice as he spoke was thoughtful.

"Centuries ago, when we were not witnesses as we have been here today, our people were removed from their homeland where they had suffered under the rule of the Roman Empire. They rose again to watch as that empire fell. History will repeat itself. I promise you here today: our people will return to their homeland."

They all stood quietly, staring out to sea. The sun was shining brightly now. Its reflection on the water around the dock was somehow calming to Benny. He was without words as he watched the movement of the waves gently lapping against the pilings.

Shlomo was staring ahead at what he thought could be two ships off in the distance. "Look, aren't those the ships?" he exclaimed.

He had everyone's attention now.

Zev's reaction was excitement: "Yes, yes, I think you're right. Look straight ahead, just before the horizon."

Zelda's voice was almost a whisper: "Oh my G—! I think you're right." She grabbed David's arm, almost throwing him off balance. "That's them!"

She was laughing and crying at the same time. It wasn't like her to lose control of her emotions like this.

They continued to stare into the distance until the two ships disappeared over the horizon. When they could no longer see the ships, they remained standing like statues, without talking. The excitement shared for a brief moment was gone; it was replaced now by a deep feeling of sadness.

As Benny continued to look out at the expanse of sea in front of him, he felt a profound sense of loss. After several moments of silence, he spoke. His voice was calm, almost as if he were thinking aloud.

"We have to know that what we said goodbye to, this morning, was a part of who we are as a people. The pain suffered by our Jewish brothers and sisters, not only the physical pain but also the pain of rejection and their disgraceful expulsion from here, from a place they believed to be their homeland, will remain as a scar on Jewish hearts everywhere for ever."

He turned, looking at David and Zev. "I shared with these people in their struggle to get here. I saw their ability to dream, their strength to overcome the challenges. I lived with these people for months. I witnessed the wedding of a couple in love during these challenges and later held their baby. I saw these people go hungry as they prayed for their dead, and I encouraged them to stay strong. I told them they were almost home. And I listened as they sang about a homeland, a homeland that rejected them."

Shlomo placed his hand on Benny's shoulder. He knew his friend was feeling the emotional pain and remorse of the last months.

Benny pointed to the mast of the *Patria* visible from the dock, protruding from its watery grave.

"More than two hundred of our people—men, women, and children—lost their lives there." He hesitated, then shook his head as if to clear it. His voice was hoarse with emotion. "This can never happen again."

David placed his hand on Benny's arm, taking his hand. "This is why we do what we do, so this will never happen again."

The docks were busy when they left. Ships were being loaded with cargoes, and there was a lot of yelling going on between dock workers. Things were back to normal, it seemed. Zev suggested having breakfast at the hotel before checking out. Everyone agreed, especially Shlomo.

They were quiet during breakfast. It was obvious everyone was still feeling the sadness from earlier. After breakfast, they said goodbye in the lobby. Arrangements were made to meet in Tel Aviv the following week. Benny and Shlomo would be going home to Yagur for now.

Home for Benny had always been Varda. He had been gone too long. He wondered if Varda would be able to see the difference in the man that left and the man he had become.

He wondered: Could he find himself again on the path he was about to enter? Only time would tell.

EPILOGUE

After their expulsion, over fifteen hundred refugees landed in Mauritius on December 28, 1940, where they would spend the next five years as prisoners of the British government. During the war with Germany, the British enlisted the help of Jewish detainees, promising freedom for all when the Germans were defeated. Many able-bodied male detainees volunteered to fight for the British against the Nazis.

The war was won. The British kept their promise. The Jewish Agency eagerly prepared for the return of their people.

On the twenty-sixth day of August, 1945, Jewish refugees left Mauritius and returned to their homeland. They were welcomed warmly by members of the Jewish Agency. Two and a half years later, they witnessed the birth of the State of Israel.

We remember these immigrants with great love, along with those who lost their lives during their pursuit of survival.

~

One hundred and twenty-seven Jewish refugees also died while in Mauritius. Their graves remain to this day in St. Martin's Cemetery.

Hatikva

As long as in the heart within,
the soul of a Jew still yearns,
and onward, towards the ends of the East,
an eye still gazes toward Zion;
our hope is not yet lost,
the two-thousand-year-old hope
to be a free nation in our land,
the land of Zion and Jerusalem.

The Young Captain on a Broken Boat is a continuation of *Pursuit of Peril* that connects the life of Isaac Adler as a baby born in Bratislava while escaping the Nazis to a British prison on the Island of Mauritius. As a young boy Isaac dreams of being rescued by a ship that will take him to Eretz Israel while playing on a broken boat half buried in the sand.

Accompanied by his drawings, written with the simplicity of a child, Isaac shares his life as that young Jewish boy. This book is a story to be shared.

Hardback ISBN: 978-1-911211-74-7

Lightning Source UK Ltd.
Milton Keynes UK
UKHW010631051121
393428UK00002B/243